The Games

Nevadaland Vol.2

by

T. N. Kaylor

The Games
Nevadaland 2

Amazon Print edition.

This is a work of fiction. Names, characters, businesses, places, events and incidents are either the products of the author's imagination or used in a fictitious manner. Any resemblance to actual persons, living or dead, or actual events is purely coincidental.

ISBN-10:
1-946948-19-5

ISBN-13:
978-1-946948-19-9

Library of Congress Control Number: 2017906419

Cover design by Gorify™.
Edited by Robert H. Kaylor.

DEDICATION

Dedicated to the silver state of Nevada, whose
fierce libertarianism inspired so much pride that I felt
compelled to write a series about being trapped
twelve and a half miles on the right side of the border.

Psst

She left a *NEVADALAND* guide for you at:
DieselDuran.com

Maps
Photos
Drawings
Guides
More

CONTENTS

The New Born

October 30, 2020.

A disturbed child too goth for his age, Angel Rodriguez stared daggers at his paramedic mother through the dirty rear window. Disgusted, he glanced at the repulsive ambulance driver further down the vinyl bench seat. The pudgy man with a blonde goatee tore open another twenty-dollar snack-bag of chile picante Corn Nuts with his gnarly teeth.

(How wasteful. I can't afford a phone, but I have to watch this guy eat money.)

"You know, Gary, those are on the excluded list," Angel said. "Along with *all* junk food."

"And that makes these babies even more freaking delicious." Enjoying the stink of fried corn and chili powder, Gary scratched his bald head and crunched on his third bag.

(Gringos and their fake Mexican junk food.)

He spoke with his mouth full, "So Angel, this is your second ride-along this week. Shouldn't you be in school?" Fugitive crumbs clung to his facial hair and nested with the others.

"It's Nevada Day, Gary. No school today." Angel looked away, disinterested.

Gary checked his watch, then sucked more Corn Nuts from the crinkly pouch. He chewed his words. "So it is. You got me there, *Chico.*"

"Stop calling me *Chico.* Both my parents were born in Nevada. And you know what? I don't even speak Spanish. But then again, neither do you, Gary."

(Dad's the bilingual one, but he's in Cali now.)

"Look kid, riding around with your beaner ass up front ain't no picnic for me neither. Why you always gotta be here? You're crimping my style."

(Style? He has got to be kidding.)

"Cramping."

"What?

"It's *cramping* my style, not 'crimping.'"

"Whatever, *Chico.* Shut up."

"Damn, Gary, I was born in Reno—not Mexico. And you know I'm only here because Mom can't afford a babysitter." Dark shaggy bangs hung in Angel's eyes as he went back to watching his mother stabilize her patient. "I'm nine now. I'll be ten in three weeks. I don't need a stupid babysitter. I can take care of myself. I don't like being stuck here with your dumb ass either—"

"Language!"

Angel huffed, "Take it up with Maria when she's done being the hero." He pointed over his shoulder toward the back of the rig.

(While you're at it, ask that bitch why she drove my dad away. All the way to Southern California. A nine-hour drive away. Truth is, Mom never leaves me alone—not even for a second—because she's afraid I'll run away to Compton to go be with Dad instead. She wants to keep me all to herself. So, go on. Ask her. I'll wait.)

In awkward silence, the driver cruised along until he exited highway I-80. In the back of the ambulance, Maria slid a needle into Eloisa Duran's arm. Then after inserting the catheter, she hung a bag of saline over the pregnant woman's stretcher and injected the IV port with three more medications. An experienced medic, Maria remained calm while working at an urgent pace. Blood dripped and pooled onto the metal floor, splattering her black sneakers. Maria spread her patient's legs, checked under her skirt, and cut off her panties. She saw the baby's head crowning. Ready or not, Diesel was on her way into the world.

"This is happening. She's in the second phase," Maria announced from under Eloisa's bloody sundress.

Angel turned to Gary and asked, "Shouldn't we use lights and sirens? And I don't know, maybe go faster?"

"You'd like that, wouldn't you, *Chico?*"

(Wow. Such a colossal asshole.)

A woman's voice squawked from the radio, "Dispatch to EMS Five, what's your twenty?"

Swallowing his half-chewed mouthful of fried corn, Gary snatched the radio mic and pressed the talk button. "EMS Five to

Dispatch. We're exiting onto Pyramid now." Gary stifled a cough as chili tickled the back of his throat.

"Interesting choice, EMS Five. Taking the scenic route?"

"Is there some sort of hurry? You got a hot date for the Bonanza tonight, Stephanie?"

"I wish."

Gary shuffled his ass and sat up straight. He lowered his voice, hoping to sound sexy, "I could make that happen Angel Face."

"No hurry. None at all. *They* have decided. Patient care is to be aborted. *They* gave the order."

Angel looked at him in disbelief.

(Aborted?)

Gary resumed his professional and detached tone. "Copy that. Abort. I'll pass on the order." He hung the mic back on its hook.

"Copy. Dispatch out."

"Hey, *Chico*, pop that window open." Gary gestured behind his head.

Angel slid open the cargo window. A monitor beeped as Eloisa's heart stopped.

Gary yelled into the back of the rig as Maria started CPR, "Hey, Maria. Abort."

The paramedic looked up from her patient in disbelief, "What?"

"We're supposed to let this one go." Keeping one eye on the road, Gary crumpled his empty snack-bag wrapper and tossed it to the floor. "*They* said to abort."

"But she's pregnant," Maria objected while continuing CPR.

"Abort. And abort, again." Gary smiled at his clever retort as he braked for a red light. "Let them both go."

Ignoring her orders, Maria slit the front of Eloisa's dress, cut her patient's bra off, and charged the defibrillator.

(I'm the hostage of a hero.)

The traffic light turned green, and Gary pulled into the parking lot of an abandoned industrial building. "I won't drive her to the hospital." He twisted his key and killed the engine. "I'm not getting into hot water over some half-dead, piece-of-crapola straggler from the wilds."

"You coward!" Maria gelled the defibrillator paddles and zapped Eloisa's heart.

"You're disobeying a direct order." Gary jumped out of the cab and hustled to the back of the rig faster than his out-of-shape body should have been able to move. Then he yanked open the double doors. "Stop *NOW!* Abort. You must allow her to terminate. *They* said so."

"Never!" Maria zapped her patient again.

"You know what *They* will do, Maria. *They* will come after *YOUR* son. *They* will take Angel."

Maria froze in place. The monitor continued its flatline tone.

Gary took the paddles from her defeated and bloody-soaked hands. Without another word, Maria tore off her blue nitrile gloves and dove into her case of meds. She drew 75 mg of morphine into an intravenous needle. Like an expert, she rolled up her left sleeve and tied a rubber tube above her bicep with one hand. Flicking the familiar vein on the inside of her elbow, she coaxed it to the surface. Then Maria injected the opiate. Within moments, all her anxiety floated away along with any care she had for anything or anyone. Every muscle in Maria's body relaxed. She reclined onto the orange vinyl bench next to the two forgotten lives on the stretcher. Gary paid no mind to Maria's inappropriate indulgence. He had seen her do this many times before.

(And now it all makes sense.)

Before she drifted away, Maria spotted Angel at the tailgate of the ambulance. For the first time, the boy had seen the truth. In a desperate attempt to distract her son, Maria pulled a loose Atomic Fireball out of her pocket and gestured at him.

"Come here, Angel."

(You always said Dad left because of drugs. You wanted me to think it was HIS drugs. But Dad left because of YOUR drugs. Didn't he? You're the junkie. All along, you've ALWAYS been the junkie. Why don't you just let me go be with Dad?)

The indignant boy climbed into the back of the ambulance and sat on his knees at his mother's feet. Fading into bliss, she held out the still-wrapped candy like Father Ortiz giving Holy communion at the Cathedral of Immaculate Conception.

(Also on the restricted list. Candy. I bet that cost a whole buck.)

Angel considered the forbidden fireball as Maria's eyes rolled back into her head. At that moment, a long-ago buried seed of darkness sprouted within him. Turning his gaze to the dead woman on the stretcher, his soul screamed anger as he remained outwardly silent and calm. Between a dead mother's still-warm legs, Diesel slithered out. Still attached, the purple preemie covered in chunky goop landed in a pile of post-mortem defecation. Three orbs of light, one yellow, one pink, and one blue, appeared and circled around the baby. The infant inhaled her first breath as the orbs flew down her throat. Then Diesel exhaled a deafening, and nearly inhuman, yowl. Both mother and daughter smelled of trauma, defeat, death, and—

(Shit.)

Enraged, Angel turned back to his mother's offering hand. He opened his mouth wide and bit down on her middle finger. Gnashing, he chewed on her until she bled. Numb and almost gone, Maria failed to react. Blood oozed into her boy's mouth as he stripped the flesh from her fingertip. Angel enjoyed the coppery taste of retribution. Then Maria passed into blissful darkness, not from the pain, but from the morphine. On autopilot and unimpressed by the energy orbs, Gary made a futile attempt to bandage the exposed bone of his partner's de-gloved finger.

"You little monster!" Gary hissed.

(You have no idea.)

A tiny wad of pink paper floated in a puddle of blood at his side. Still chewing, Angel snatched the Post-It Note, got up off his knees, swallowed his snack, and walked away. He admired the way crimson soaked into the ragged and dirty edges of the note as he picked at it. He smoothed out the paper and read the blood-smeared blue scribbled message aloud, "You have to play to lose."

(Someone thinks they're clever.)

Casually, he strolled toward home. Using the well-worn creases, he folded the note in half, then in half again, then shoved it into his pocket. Alone and lost in thoughtlessness, he felt slightly high, almost happy—in a totally nihilistic way. Things would never be the same between Angel and his mother ever again. And even though he had no way of knowing it, he would cross paths with that new born again one day.

The Junkie

April 1, 2037.

Bull sprinted toward the barracks with Diesel slung over his left shoulder. Walker galloped along-side, pressing on her torn stump with his palm. Blood gushed down his forearm. Juggling her severed leg, Cheng tightened the belt wrapped around her thigh as a tourniquet.

"Put more pressure on it," Bull barked at Walker. "Put *MORE* pressure *ON* it."

Cheng adjusted his sunglasses.

Groggy, Diesel awoke and muttered to herself, "It's the bride. She's dead. She's bloody. From the Bonanza. She's come for me."

Like a ghost, the blood-soaked bride with beautiful long platinum hair glided behind Bull, smiling at Diesel like a loving mother.

Diesel lifted her head, "Amelia? Is that you?"

"I come when needed."

No one heard the ghost except Diesel.

"You are going to be all right." Cheng attempted eye contact over his sunglasses, but her gaze was fixed on something else— nothing.

Their collars all pulsed.

"One minute," Cheng announced.

Diesel winked at her invisible friend. "But *you* don't wear a collar, right, Amelia?"

The bloody bride smiled and nodded with approval.

"Because you're dead," Diesel mumbled as she dropped her head.

"Amelia?" Confused, Cheng repeated the word into his glasses and got no translation.

As a frantic cluster, the friends sprinted for the courtyard. Limp again, Diesel's head bobbed upside-down against Bull's back. She slipped, and he tightened his grip around her hips. Inside the safe zone, players hunched over and gasped for breath. Other bloody blue-collars sprinted in from all angles. The gang of reluctant friends made it across the finish line with a few seconds to spare, just as exhibition alarm sounded.

"That's the end," Bull said without slowing down. He kept running. On the outside of the line, four collars detonated. Heads exploded into gore chunks. Arterial spray shot fast and hard into the air like blood geysers. Decapitated bodies ran into the courtyard until each one collapsed like a sack of wet potatoes. Drones broadcasted every glorious second of the slaughter, but the friends ignored the carnage show behind them. Bull kicked open the barracks door and dashed inside.

"Where are you going?" Walker struggled to keep up.

"I know a guy," Bull said.

"Keep putting pressure on it," Cheng said while squeezing through the hall.

"I am. I am putting pressure on it."

"Wh-what happened?" Diesel asked.

"You had an accident, Diesel. You are going to be all right," Cheng said.

Bull kicked in a dorm room door. Inside, he found the assless chicken man bent over the bottom bunk.

"Get your black ass out of my face," Bull sneered.

At the sound of the boot's voice, the yellow chicken raised his wings, stood up straight, and backed away from the bed. Exposed, Angel Rodriguez fussed and tucked before jumping out of the bottom bunk. He ran a nervous hand through his dark, shoulder-length hair. The chicken made a dash for the window.

"Freeze, Chickenman!" Bull ordered with authority.

Angel replied, "What the hell?"

Bull laid Diesel on the bottom bunk. Blood sprayed everywhere. The ghost bride stepped forward to shower in the red glory. She tilted her head upward and let Diesel's blood rain into her mouth.

"My leg. It's my leg," Diesel groaned.

"Jesus!" Angel said. "Put her legs up. Put her legs up."

Confused, Cheng raised the severed leg over his head, but no one noticed his mistake. Bull shoved pillows under Diesel's stumped thigh and propped her other leg up on the bed frame. He grabbed the raw meat of her leg and pressed on her severed artery.

"How much blood has she lost?" Angel asked.

"A lot," Walker said.

Sweaty and pale, Diesel rolled her head back and forth. Her body trembled. "It hurts. My leg. Oh. *OH*. It *HURTS*!"

"Don't look at it," Walker said to Diesel.

Cheng hid Diesel's severed limb behind his back so that she wouldn't see it.

"Help," Diesel whimpered. "Help me."

The bloody bride wrapped her arm around Walker and rested her head on his shoulder like they were best friends. Of course, Walker didn't notice, because he couldn't see or feel Amelia.

"Hook her up, Angel," Bull ordered.

"What? I don't know what you mean." Angel glanced at the chicken man.

"Cut the shit and give her some drugs!" Bull yelled.

Diesel groaned in pain.

Angel nodded at his chicken-dressed drug dealer. The reg' popped his hand out of a wing-hole and reached into his rear access opening.

"Wait. Why are you wearing latex gloves?" Bull asked.

Chickenman shrugged.

"You know what? I don't want to know. Just hand over the drugs."

The drug dealer pulled a loaded syringe from a hidden internal pocket near the small of his back and handed the heroin to Angel. Snatching his belt from the floor, Angel wrapped it around Diesel's upper arm. He tightened the buckle. Like an expert, Angel injected her with the pain medication.

Diesel stopped trembling and relaxed.

Angel gestured at Cheng. "In my sock drawer, there's a medical kit. A black zipper bag. Bring it to me."

Diesel's breathing went from labored to shallow as shock took over. Then she lost consciousness again. Cheng sat Diesel's leg on the dresser and rummaged around in the drawer. After he found the doctor's bag, he tossed it to Angel. The once-upon-a-time paramedic caught and opened his medical kit without a word. He pulled out a hemostat. He touched Bull on the arm to dismiss him.

"I got this."

Bull let go, and blood pumped slowly out of Diesel's thigh again. Angel pinched her femoral artery closed with the hemostat. He tore open a pouch of saline and washed away the blood on her torn quadriceps. Then he examined the trauma. "Jesus, she needs a hospital. A surgeon. I'm just an out-of-practice medic."

"A junkie medic," Bull added.

"A junkie medic who wouldn't be stuck here if it weren't for you," Angel snarled in Bull's face.

"*They* will never let us go to a hospital," Walker said, ignoring the hostility between the men.

"He's right," Bull agreed.

"I can patch her up. I have some unexpired antibiotics I saved for an emergency. In my supply stash." Angel pointed at his foot locker. Then he looked at the assless chicken man, "But she needs blood."

Even though blood soaked the room, Chickenman looked terrified when he heard the word spoken aloud. "Hey, yeah, sure I can get things. But I get street things like guns and drugs. Man, I can't get blood. Nope. No way. Not fast, anyway. Shit like that takes time. Dangerous freaks run the blood game. I'd have to find the right people and make a whole new batch of friends. That's a serious investment of time with an unlikely payoff," the chicken man vamped from behind his rubber beak.

"I am a universal donor." Cheng stepped forward and volunteered his arm. "Give her my blood."

May 1, 2037. The Last Exhibition.

Leading the excursion, Walker popped open a padlock, removed a chain, and opened the rusty shed door. Stale dust and musty darkness hit him in the face. Walker stepped inside and yanked on the grimy string of the single, bare lightbulb. Alerted by the light, a rat scurried off the workbench and disappeared into a crack in the wall.

Cheng and Angel followed Walker. Diesel hobbled behind on crutches the guys had made from a broken bunk bed ladder. After she stepped inside, a gust of wind caught the door and slammed it behind her.

Squinting in the low light, Walker pawed at Cheng's shades, "Take those off, man."

In one, smooth motion, Cheng blocked and swatted him away. "Do *NOT* touch my sunglasses."

"Hmphf." Walker gathered a drop cloth that covered the lump on the workbench to reveal a mechanical prosthetic. Both crude and impressive, this custom-built robot leg dazzled everyone. Diesel gasped. She tossed her crutches against the wall and hopped over to the work bench.

"You weren't kidding. It's amazing, Walker!"

"Thanks, Diesel."

"I'm more and more impressed by ULCER every day." Diesel examined the spring-like tension foot. She lifted the prosthetic. "Wow, it's lighter than I expected."

"Titanium," Walker said with pride.

"You must tell me where you found titanium." Discreetly, Cheng took a series of photos with his sunglasses.

"I have my ways." Acting like a magician, he flung another drop cloth aside. A series of weaponized attachments lined the bench in a neat row, each holstered inside a custom-molded slot of a leather sling.

"Whoa," Angel said.

Walker removed the accessory that looked like a lobster claw and held it up to the light. "The weapons interchange at an artificial knee joint. We built a socket into a harness that this—" He pointed to the hip-type ball on the end, "Locks into." After sliding the attachment back into the holster, he stepped aside and offered the rig to Diesel.

Still holding her runner extension, Diesel spun on her toes. She placed the accessory in its slot so she could examine each of her new leg-tools. The first had a circular saw blade where her foot would have been. "For cutting," she said. The lobster claw made her smile again. "For crushing." And the last, but not the least, the third attachment looked like an oversized praying mantis pincer. "For…" Diesel ran her fingertips along the serrated edges and then touched the sharp tip. Her pupils dilated. "For I don't know what yet. But I sure like it."

(I love these guys.)

"How did you engineer all this in just a month?" she asked.

"I was wondering the same thing," Cheng said.

"Never mind all that. Let's get you fitted before the exhibition ends." Walker gestured for Angel's help and tossed two clasps and a hammer onto the work bench. Diesel climbed onto the sturdy table as her friends huddled around. She unpinned her cutoff pant-leg. The guys drilled, soldered, ratcheted, and clamped the cup socket to custom fit it to her stump. Walker buckled a leather garter belt over her cargo pants. He fastened two titanium bars that flanked each side of her thigh and then attached to her cup socket. Cheng tightened an additional leather strap high-inside her thigh to add stability.

"How does that feel?" Cheng asked.

(That feels… Good. Really good. Like sexy good.)

Self-conscious, Diesel blushed and nodded. Angel tugged on the security rig and gave the guys a thumbs up. Walker opened the lever, slid the ball joint into her thigh cup, closed the lever, and locked it. The guys stepped back, and Diesel stretched out her leg to admire the running attachment. She hopped down from the workbench and paced in a circle. Her infectious smile grew with each step.

Testing, she balanced her weight on each foot. She bounced back and forth from one foot to the prosthetic and back. Thrilled to see her mobile again, the guys all smiled. Walker held out her gadget holster like an overcoat. Diesel threaded her arms through each strap and hitched the custom pack onto her back. Cheng helped her attach the buckles and secured her holster. During the fitting, his hands brushed her breast by accident, and while Cheng didn't notice, Diesel almost lost her cool.

(Damn, that feels good. What's wrong with me?)

"How does that fit?" Cheng asked.

Shy, Diesel blushed red and nodded again. She couldn't speak.

"That is your default." Walker pointed to her artificial foot. "That is the same model disabled Olympian runners use. The handicapped can actually beat able-bodied athletes with that attachment."

"Disabled?" Diesel jumped and kicked to display her impressive abilities. "I'm not handicapped. I'm bionic. I'm weaponized. I'm more *abled* than ever."

"Sorry, Diesel. Poor choice of words," Walker said. "The saw runs on gasoline. We went with gas, since we didn't know if you'd be able to charge batteries once the games start. So plan accordingly."

"Got it." Diesel nodded.

"The saw uses gasoline for fuel, the same way that the word 'diesel' means fuel. Is that not considered poetic? Or would that be ironic?" Cheng asked.

Angel laughed. "I suppose so."

"Well there's a self-fulfilling prophecy if I've ever seen one," Walker said.

Cheng checked his glasses for the definition of 'self-fulfilling prophecy.'

"So, isn't this cheating? I thought each player could have one, and only one, weapon in the games," Diesel said.

Angel answered, "*They* don't care what we do. We can hide. We can kill. We can cheat—"

"I know all about your cheating," Diesel interrupted. "I never told you. But I watched that fake fight against the stereotype street thugs back during training. A gang banger with a switchblade? Come on. Even I know that's a ridiculous cliché, and I don't watch television. You did all that to pump up your numbers."

"So? Does it matter? No. As long as everyone keeps watching and betting, *They* leave us be," Angel replied. "The more horrible we are to each other the more money *They* make. The more money *They* make, the more we get away with."

"And I thought Walker was the cynical one," Diesel said.

Walker laughed off Angel's remarks while pointing at her leg rig, "Let's just call this a loophole."

"Okay. I get it. We're just 'leveling the playing field.'" Angel's comment dripped with sarcasm. "I like that. Besides, who cares if she cheats?"

"I do." Diesel meant it.

"Someday, you will get over that neurosis," Cheng said.

"Anyway..." Not liking the direction the conversation had taken, Walker continued with his tutorial, "And with the claw and mantis, you'll need to practice. If you flex your quads, the pinchers will close." He mimicked a lobster claw opening and closing with his hand. "Those attachments are pneumatic. I'll help you learn. But for now, we should head back to the barracks so we don't run out of time."

"We want no more accidents," Cheng said.

"No more accidents," Diesel repeated. She dropped into an impressive handstand, took a few steps with her hands, flipped into a backbend, stuck the landing, and stood gracefully. Then she exclaimed with attitude, "Now *that's DEE*-lux."

The Bloody Bride

August 23, 2035.

At age fourteen, Diesel had completely recovered from her involuntary surgery. Every morning, when she showered and dressed, the two tiny purple scars on each side of her belly button reminded her of waking up in the hospital after the boots took her away. A year ago today, she got her first menstrual period. That one had also been her last.

(Now, I have no uterus. No ovaries. No hormones. THEY spayed me like some house cat and left me with forever-tiny boobs that will never grow. And a figure like a beanpole. I'm closer to being the boy THEY always said I was. And the worst part is, I don't even care.)

The space-scape filled every inch of wall, ceiling, and floor. Months ago, she had lifted and rolled back the corner of the carpet to expose a fresh concrete canvas. Over time, she tore out the entire rug and padding, then shoved the rolled wads under her bed. She finished painting the floor a few weeks ago and without room to expand her mural, the hotel room felt more and more like a prison.

(I can only look at it now.)

Yesterday, she moved her bed to the middle of the room and surrounded it with a moat of stacked hotel furniture. She stowed that annoying flatscreen television under the bed with the rolled carpet.

(I don't want anything to block my view of home.)

Dressed and ready, she waited in a steady handstand on top the shortest dresser and stared at her painted lava flow upside-down.

(How do I get from here to there?)

At six a.m. her door automatically unlocked. Diesel flipped off the dresser and stuck the landing on snowdrift-painted concrete. She sprinted out her unlocked door, down the dim hallway, and to the bank of elevators. Tapping her sneaker against the tile floor, she pressed the down button. It lit. The ticking numbers over the closed brass elevator doors stopped at each and every level while creeping downward. Six more wards wandered into the lobby to wait with her.

(Everyone's trying to get out at the same time. The car's gonna be packed. Every day with this shit. Screw it.)

Diesel pushed through the growing crowd as more and more wards crammed into the lobby. She ran down the hall and slammed open the door to the stairwell. After dashing down several flights of steps, she interrupted some boys smoking contraband. Guilty, the kids hid the cigarettes behind their backs.

"As you were." Disinterested, she ran past the guys.

With only two flights to go, she found a crinkled postcard in the center of a landing. She stopped and stared at it between her feet.

(This wasn't here yesterday.)

Diesel squatted. She poked at the frayed edges and dog-eared corners of the postcard. Age had worn the gloss away. The browned photo of Slots-O-Fun looked like the fake vintage photos that tourists posed for in Ye Old-Tyme Westerns on the Promenade downstairs. She picked up the card and flipped it over. In the corner, a postmark from Las Vegas canceled a vintage ten-cent stamp. On the left, black felt-tipped handwriting smeared and faded across the yellowing card stock. Water spots polka-dotted the message.

[February 14, 1979. My darling Samuel, I waited for you at the (blurred) chapel, my love. I fret over whatever has delayed you, for I know deep in my heart that you would never leave me at the altar. Even if (blurred) said so. We've waited our whole lives to be together, and so I can (blurred) a little (blurred.) I pray this message reaches you safe and sound. Forever yours, Amelia]

Realizing she'd been holding her breath while reading, Diesel gasped. A bead of sweat rolled down the back of her neck. Her hands trembled. When she exhaled, her breath turned into fog. She shivered. A compulsion took over as she focused on the return address on the right.

(I must write back to her. NOW.)

May 4, 2037.

The bloody bride walked through the wall of the horse stable. "Miss Duran. I'm your Nevadaland appointed guardian." The ghost appeared where *Green Room #4* had been stenciled over aged wood.

(Why so formal? You know my name.)

Diesel touched the white-washed letter *G* next to Amelia's transparent head.

(Wet paint.)

Cheng paced around the half-dozen other players in the stall. Passing by Diesel, he smiled. Then he joined a conversation between Walker and Bull while keeping an eye on her.

(Guardian? No one else has a guardian. Not one that I can see, anyway. I get a raving axe-killer ghost as a guardian? How's that supposed to help?)

"My name is Amelia."

"Yeah, I know," Diesel whispered. Self-conscious, she grinned back at Cheng. She kicked a pile of hay with her prosthetic leg while mumbling to herself, "Smells like piss."

(Do these guys see you? Am I losing it? If you think I'm going to talk to you while other players are here, you're not just crazy, you're stupid.)

The ghost bride continued, "It's time."

Everyone's blue collars flashed white.

Amelia vanished. She just faded away.

(Why the hell did she do that? It's been over a year since I talked with her. And now she shows up to say some weird shit and disappear. I don't get it. What's the point?)

Amelia popped her head back through the wall, "The point is— I'm on stand by. I'll be here if you need me. Why can't you let me be all dramatic? I mean, shit. I'm *DEAD*. What's the fun in being a ghost if I can't act all spooky and mysterious? You make me spell out everything. That's so—pedestrian."

"Who said death should be fun?" Diesel asked.

Annoyed, Amelia disappeared again.

Techno music blared. An eager crowd of orange-collared regs' in the arena cheered for the choreographed lines of beauties dancing on stage. Each hopeful wore a pink one-piece bathing suit with silver trim. Glittery silver tap shoes emphasized every perfectly timed step as the girls performed funky synchronized spins and jazzy high kicks. Hip grinding and shoulder shaking punctuated each move, turning the routine into a seductive tease— without the stripping. A swarm of drones swirled overhead, filling the night sky while flashing pink and blue lights in time with the music.

No longer needing the rope to keep them in line, the players marched in from the stables and waited behind the black curtain.

Walker stretched his arms wide. "This is the big show."

"Dozens of players have died already." Diesel tightened her thigh strap. "Or been injured."

"That is how the games go," Cheng said.

"So, how do the beauties get eliminated?" Diesel asked.

"Beauties don't get eliminated," Bull said.

"Well, that doesn't seem fair." Diesel tugged at her too-tight tank top to stretch it out. "So much for equality."

"So what's going on there?" Walker pointed at her chest. "It's like your boobs grew in overnight. Guess you're a late bloomer."

"Don't *you* worry about *my* blooms." Diesel pushed her breasts up and let them flop inside her top.

(Even with all this, THEY still won't give me a bra.)

"See? Competition makes girls bitch—" He glanced at Diesel. "I mean, snippy." Walker ducked and tied the laces of his tactical boot.

"No. Competition makes the winning beauties even more precious," Bull said.

"Sure, if you dig trophy wives." Walker retied his other shoe.

Puzzled, Cheng read the search results inside his glasses. "If they become slaves for life, I fail to see the female advantage?"

"Girls' heads don't explode if they don't make it to the Coliseum in time," Walker said. "That's a clear advantage."

"Unfair!" Diesel said. "Loser girls get to live, while players die. I'm on the wrong team!"

Bull pointed through the curtain at an attractive young woman selling beer in the bleachers. "Losing pink-collars become society's servants. Waitresses, cooks, housekeepers. You know, the yellow-collars."

"I started out as a yellow-collar." Diesel crossed her arms to cover her chest.

"Yes," Bull agreed. "Yellow collars really are the lowest class."

Flirting, Diesel swatted his thick bicep. "Asshole." She giggled.

"I wasn't kidding. I'd rather be a homeless reg' than a yellow-collar."

His careless comment forced Diesel to retreat.

(Asshole.)

The friends craned their necks to peek through the curtain. Diesel spotted her old friend, Chelsea Carter.

(She's Chelsea DUPONT now, and she's such an amazing dancer. I sure miss her.)

Off to the side, a couple reg' street-bookies stood on the roof of a baseball dugout. The bookkeepers used the scoreboard to post the latest beauty and player stats. Scrambling to place one more bet, Regs' pushed each other down the bleachers. Others fought while hanging over the rails to get a last chance at the bookies.

(Chaos. The new normal.)

Cheng noticed Diesel staring. He explained the gambling rules. "This is their final opportunity for a wager. Once the games begin, *They* take no new bets."

Two black-collars on headsets passed, talking to each other, "Rowdy crowd this year."

"That makes for great television," one guy said.

Grabbing the smaller crew member by the arm, Bull interrupted. "Hey, fella, I don't like being without my sword."

"Nobody has a weapon here, player. You're safe." The crew member slipped from Bull's grasp.

Bull gestured at Diesel's leg gadget pack strapped to her back. "She's got her weapons."

"Hey!"

(He snitched on me. That's two disses in the last two minutes. What the hell?)

"She is a loophole. You leave her alone." Cheng put his arm around Diesel and pulled her away from the conversation.

Bull laughed at everyone, then raised his voice, "Do you *KNOW* how many enemies I have? How many people that are dying to take a shot at me? I'm *never* safe." The crew member walked away from Bull's tantrum, but the angry player yanked him back by his black collar. "I do *NOT* like being unarmed. Or ignored."

A drone spotted the altercation. At once, Bull's collar turned red, vibrated, and got hot. Bull dropped the guy, and he scurried away. The drone hovered for a few seconds. Once satisfied, it flew off to join the others in the swarm over the stage. Bull's collar switched from red to blue.

"That shit won't happen once I become a gladiator."

Meanwhile on the other side of the curtain, the pink-collar dancers shook their money-makers as more regs' filled the cheap seats in the nosebleed section. Always embittered, Krissi Christmas tripped Chelsea, but no one noticed except Diesel.

(That bitch!)

Without falling, Chelsea recovered and stepped right back into the routine like nothing happened. Krissi scowled. Diesel clapped with enthusiasm.

Meanwhile, everyone else fixated on the gladiators. Battle armor rattled as the warriors entered the arena. The crowd went wild each time a hero appeared from the tunnel under the bleachers. Regs' hung over the rails to high-five the gladiators jogging beneath. Then, over two-feet taller than the others, Kali stomped through.

An eager 'reg dangled by his feet, held by a friend. The fan managed to touch Kali's hair. Growling, the goddess spun around and slapped him with two of her right hands at once. Her claws sunk into the side of the man's face and tore bloody trenches. Blood gushed. Panicking, his friend lifted his buddy into the bleachers. With the biggest smile ever, the fan held his shredded face together with the palms of his hands.

"She touched me!" The groupie yelled into the crowd. "Did you all see that? Kali touched *ME*."

The white-collared gladiators marched on the red carpet through the rodeo arena, then climbed a few risers and flanked each side of the stage. The beauties fell into splits, rolled on the stage, and humped the floor. In the stands, reg' fans danced, clapped, and waved signs and banners for their favorite gladiators. The dancers worked the crowd into a frenzy as a faceless announcer's voice boomed through the sound system.

"And now. The producer of the games. And everyone's favorite showman, the Master."

All the dancers dropped into a kneeling position. Beauty hands slapped the stage in unison. Then the girls touched their foreheads to the floor. The crowd stood and cheered with wild applause. The regs' whistled and hooted for the Master as he appeared from the same tunnel as the gladiators.

"Thank *YOU*," the Master broadcasted into a bullhorn that blasted into his microphone. "*YOU* are *ALL* winners!" In his expensive purple suit and subtle platform boots, the Master strutted down the red carpet like a pimp-gameshow host. A cameraman sitting on a crane zoomed overhead and captured a close-up of the Master's gilded-cage top hat. A snow cricket hopped around inside the fine golden mesh, creaking its hind legs together.

The Master pointed into the lens, stuck his face in front of the camera, and proclaimed to everyone watching at home, "I love each and every one of *YOU! YOU* are *ALL* winners!"

The Master left the videographer and stepped onto the stage, absorbing more applause with every step. He hurried his pace as he passed Kali, not out of fear, but because she stood almost four feet taller than him. To preserve his larger-than-life persona, he always minimized onscreen time shared with the goddess. The hopeful dancers formed an adoring gauntlet as the girls pointed to a pedestal upstage. The Master climbed stairs to a platform that raised him high above everyone else. When he got to the top, he shushed the crowd.

The applause stopped and everyone took their seats. All betting stopped. All the drones shined little white lights on the Master. As silence fell over the packed-to-capacity arena, everyone held their breath—waiting for him to say the words.

The Master tilted his head back and pointed his bullhorn high. He stretched his microphone far and wide to look mighty and massive. Then he said it. He said the words. He said, "Let the games begin!"

The crowd erupted with insane adulation.

Following black-collar guides, weaponless players spilled out from behind the curtain, around the base of the Master's pedestal, and through the gauntlet of hopefuls. The men charged down the steps past the gladiators. The leading black-collars blocked the tunnel exit and pointed left, down the horse track, instead.

"Take a lap!" The regs' chanted over and over. "Take a lap. Take a lap."

The players jogged around the stadium while waving at adoring fans. Diesel kept up the pace with her running attachment, impressing everyone.

"You're like poor little tink-tink," Walker said, struggling to keep up with her. "Running on an aluminum boomerang."

Clueless, Diesel shrugged.

"You know, Kat Williams the comedian? Stand up?" Walker looked for validation from other runners. He got none. "It's like you're running on a paper clip. Get it? 'Tink. Tink.' It's comedy. Damn."

Diesel shrugged again and kept going. Cheng approached her other side.

"Look at the girly gimp," a fat, middle-aged reg' heckled while pointing at her.

Like hyenas, more regs' threw insults. A woman in her late 70's with frizzed-out and jet-black dyed hair yelled, "You'll be the next to die, cripple girl."

Running faster, Diesel frowned, leaving Walker behind. Cheng kept pace with her. The abuse followed through the stands like a wave. Halfway around the track, some school kids busted out in cruel laughter. The jerks threw a red-and-white striped box of popcorn at Diesel. It pelted her in the head. To avoid being pummeled, Diesel switched to the innermost lane.

Cheng blocked the booing crowd by taking the next outermost lane. "We are almost there."

Tears welled up in her eyes. Diesel focused on her breathing and pace.

(In. Out. In. Out. In. Out.)

More vicious regs' jeered, but she didn't hear the crowd anymore. All she heard was air flowing through her lungs. As the players approached the end, black-collars blocked all lanes and flagged the players toward the tunnel. Diesel sprinted the last hundred yards and ducked away from the hateful crowd. She disappeared into the same tunnel from where the celebrities had emerged earlier.

(Hell on Earth.)

Cheng followed. Halfway through the tunnel, she stopped and bent over to catch her breath.

"Are you all right?"

"What is *WRONG* with people?" She huffed and puffed.

"I wish I knew, Diesel."

Inside the arena, the gladiators broke out in a sham fight to entertain the masses. Kali wrestled a tattooed muscle-man with a thick brown beard. The crowd went wild. The other gladiators joined in, starting a multi-ring Royal Rumble. Outside, crew members received the players and filed them into idling tour busses.

"What the hell?" Diesel asked. "Now what?"

"*They* cannot let us start the games here." Cheng tapped his glasses.

"*They* don't let anyone cross into the Coliseum for a month anyway. It wouldn't be much of a show if we just walked out of the arena and marched right across the finish line." Bull pulled a rolled bandage out of his pocket and wrapped his wrists in a criss-cross pattern.

"*They* have to make us fight for it," Cheng added.

Panting, Walker caught up with his friends. "Damn, you'd think I'd be in better shape by now." He sucked air. "*They* are going to dump us on the far side of the zone. Where the beasts are. Because *They* are sadistic sonofabitch monsters. And *They* know exactly what the home viewers need to stay pacified."

"Personally, I love a good challenge." Bull stomped up the bus steps and took the last seat in the back. "Let's *DO* this!"

"*They* have to make this as hard as possible, don't *They*?" Diesel plopped into the seat beside Bull.

He spoke loud enough for the whole bus to hear, "As soon as we step off this bus, I better get my damn sword back. And you all better be ready, because that's when the games truly begin."

September 9, 2035.

Someone slid something under her door. Diesel jumped off her bed.

(I miss Ernesta everyday. The new housekeeper. This third one. She doesn't even talk to me. The last time she bothered to come into my room, she acted like I was contagious or something.)

"Nope. Not contagious. Just an unwanted orphan living off the system."

Diesel ran to the locked door, and she spotted it. A glossy photo of impressive water fountains in Las Vegas. A postcard. An answer to the one she sent a couple weeks ago. She froze.

(My first piece of mail. No one has ever mailed me anything before.)

This sudden newness in her dull routine made her remember her first Christmas present so many years ago. She choked back a tear.

(What did THEY do to Ernesta?)

Just for fun, Diesel dropped down on all fours and crawled to the postcard. Rather than pick it up, she did a pushup over the card. Her biceps grew harder as she held her face close enough to read. The fancy font text said, "The Bellagio."

(I have no idea what that means, but it sure looks fancy.)

Rolling over, she snatched the card, flipped it over, and read it while lying on the floor. The hand-addressed card was postmarked a week earlier in Las Vegas, Nevada. Only three words filled the left side.

[I am DEAD.]

Spooked, Diesel threw the message at the wall. It spun and fluttered through the air. Her heart pounded. The glossy Bellagio photo smacked into her levitating mag-train mural, then landed on the floor.

"I waited in Vegas—there in that desert shithole—for nine years," a voice said from inside her room.

Diesel shrieked as she jumped straight up and grasped at her flat chest. Her heart pounded. She backed against the mural and slid along the wall for a better, yet distant, view of the room. After side shuffling, Diesel saw the bloody bride for the first time.

(She looks so sad.)

Diesel locked eyes with the spirit. Brilliant red contrasted with her pure white gown and long platinum hair. Her pale skin seemed cold and her lips were tinted cyanotic blue.

"Faithfully, I waited for him." The bride ignored the narrow path between stacked furniture and walked through the armoire before sitting on the edge of Diesel's bed. "On the tenth anniversary of being—abandoned. I... I don't know. I lost my temper."

"Are you Amelia?"

"Yes. I am Amelia. Are you Diesel?"

"Yes." She took a few steps closer. "What happened to you?"

"Ten years. I heard nothing from Samuel. Not one word. Every year on our day, I got dressed in my gown. This gown." Amelia smoothed her hand over the blood-stained taffeta. "I got dressed in *this* gown, just like all the years before, and I went to the chapel to meet Samuel. And I don't know what happened, but that time, something snapped... Inside me." The bride hung her head low in shame. Her hair draped forward and hid her alabaster face. "Yet another wedding went on in *our* space, just like every year before.

Except this time, I watched from the vestibule, and I—I grabbed an axe. And I got a little choppy."

"There was an axe in the lobby of a wedding chapel?"

The bride snapped her head back and snarled at Diesel. "All right! I brought the damn axe to the chapel. Samuel needed to be taught a lesson!"

Diesel took three steps backward to put as much distance between herself and the jilted bride as possible. Watching for sudden moves from the despondent woman, Diesel asked, "Why are you here, Amelia?"

"Why are *YOU*?" the ghost challenged back.

"I have no choice. I can't leave. I'm trapped here," Diesel answered.

"Me too. I've been stuck in Vegas since the police shot me in the chapel over fifty years ago." Amelia parted the blonde hair over her ear to show the blasted out exit wound, then covered her shattered skull again. "And you're the first person to talk to me since my death."

Diesel relaxed a bit. "Okay. So you're dead, and you're here now. What does that *mean?*"

"I don't know, but let's be friends."

The Beast

June 3, 2037.

"This will be our last chance to escape." Cheng poked at the fluffy seeds of red fountaingrass with his odd short-staff.

(He's been whittling that all month.)

A chain of dragons swallowing each other's tails crawled from the ivory handle and twisted around the curved stick.

"I'm ready to make the run for the Coliseum." Diesel pointed in the opposite direction. "If we go that way, we can get a head start. We'd be first to cross the finish line."

Walker laughed. "Right. As if everyone else hasn't already thought of that. Our good friend Bull is probably there right now, battling every single contender like the giant walking target that he is. Trust me. You do not want to be in the middle of that war zone right now."

"See that's the thing." Diesel balanced on her tink-tink and kicked a rock with her real foot. "I thought this was called 'The Games.' We've been out here hiding for almost a month, and I haven't been in a single fight yet. The only game we're playing is hide-and-seek."

"We have not fought yet because we stopped consorting with Bull," Cheng said.

"Well, actually, *HE* left *us*." Diesel flipped a double cartwheel on the riverbank of the flooded Truckee and stuck the landing.

(Damn. I love doing tricks on this thing.)

She slid her attachment backpack into place and tightened the leather straps.

"Bull attracts trouble," Cheng said. "He left us because he wanted to fight, and we got in his way. Trust me. The fewer conflicts in which we engage, the better. We need to save our strength for the gladiators."

"I don't know. I kinda like the guy," Diesel said.

"You like him? He is dangerous. He has a hunger. Once the blood flows he cannot pay attention to anything else."

"What do you expect from a boot?" Walker asked. "*They* recruit guys like that for a reason."

Cheng stopped. "You *knew* he was a boot?"

"Well, yeah. Didn't you?"

Diesel jumped back into the conversation. "Bull's a boot? No way!"

"He *WAS* a boot," Walker corrected. "We worked in the same government building years ago. Then later, he became a police officer. Then when—" Walker gestured at the landscape. "This became Nevadaland. He became a boot."

"He seems so nice."

Cheng choked on his saliva. "Bull is not a 'nice' person, Diesel."

"Why do you say that?"

"He is a bad guy. Just trust me on this."

"How'd he wind up in the games?" Diesel asked. "Did he mess up? Did Bull fail?"

(I've seen what happens to those who fail.)

"Who knows—" Walker spotted a radio tower with a blue light at the top and sprinted for it. He yelled back as he ran, "We've reached the edge. The perimeter of the zone. It's here."

After his 100-yard dash, Walker froze. Catching up, Diesel and Cheng flanked him on each side. Standing in a row, the friends stared up at the blue light in awe.

"I have not been on the other side of the zone in almost four years," Cheng said.

"This won't work." Diesel tugged on her blue collar. "These contraptions know when we go somewhere we shouldn't."

(Like when I lost my leg.)

"The water might interfere with the signal. I'm thinking if we dunk under, the collars won't be able to transmit. Call it a glitch." Walker untied and yanked off his boots. He crammed his socks into his shoes, then tied the laces together and slung the whole mess around his neck. "It's worth a test."

(Yeah. Well your last "test" didn't work out so great for me.)

Diesel crossed her arms and stepped back, "I'm not convinced."

Walker waded into the river.

"This is a horrid idea. Cheng, tell him this is a bad idea."

"I think she has a point, Walker. What makes you so sure your collar will not detonate?" Cheng poked the surface of the water with his dragon staff making ripples.

"The water." Shin-deep, Walker slogged toward the tower.

"Water? So what? Our collars still work in the rain. In the shower. In the tub. Let's just go to the Coliseum. Walker! Stop! Please, don't," Diesel pleaded from the riverbank, nearly crying.

Less than twenty feet from the blue tower and hip-deep, Walker kept going. Curious, Cheng followed along, but ten feet behind, on dry land. Anticipating disaster, Diesel backed further away. Everyone tensed up with anticipation, even Walker.

"Is it worth losing your head?" Diesel screamed at him. "Walker!"

"Yes, Diesel," Walker said with his eyes fixed on the imaginary boundary only a few feet away. "Without question, I will always risk death for a chance to escape."

A waterproof submarine drone emerged from beneath the surface and hovered in front of Walker's face. "Halt, player. Do not proceed."

Surprised, Walker flinched backward, and then his collar turned red. It vibrated. It heated.

"You are in danger of non-compliance," the drone warned.

"We are defeated, Walker. Come back now." Cheng crouched down.

"He's right." Diesel ducked further upstream.

Threatening to bump him in the head, the drone buzzed closer to Walker.

"Shit," Walker jumped back to dodge the drone hit. He turned and ran for land, but two feet deep in water, he just splashed in slow motion. His collar stayed red and got hotter. "Get back. Get *BACK!*"

Cheng scooped up a fistful of mud and pitched it at the drone. The sludge clogged one of the four propellers, sinking that corner. Still, the drone wobbled after Walker as he scrambled up the riverbank onto dry land. With lightning quick speed, Cheng attacked the amphibious drone and beat it with his stick. Walker's collar turned blue and stopped vibrating.

"Damn, you killed it." Walker clutched his cooling compliance collar.

Curious, Diesel approached. "More like pulverized it. But why, Walker? Why'd you risk it?"

"We have to find a weakness in the system. Either we hack a halo. Or find a glitch. Or crack the network. We have to find something. We have to try, while there's still time. We have to keep doing penetration tests. No system is perfect. I know for a fact that this one isn't. We have to find a weakness and exploit it."

"That sounds all righteous and noble, but how many more legs." She pointed at her stump. "Or heads, will get blown off to achieve this?"

"This is war. There will be casualties."

"Are we at war?" Cheng asked.

"We certainly are. It may still be a cold war, but it won't take much to go hot. It could be any random event."

"A catalyst," Diesel said.

"Yes. And I don't want to be stuck with one of these damn things around my neck when the first shots get fired," Walker said.

"None of us want to wear the collar, but the poor must suffer," Cheng said.

"While the strong do whatever *They* can to stay in power."

"That doesn't seem fair. It's just not right," Diesel said.

"'As the world goes—only questions between equals in power,' so said Thucydides." Walker sat on the riverbank and put his boots back on. "And we are nowhere near equal. We don't get to question what *They* determine is right."

"Is that why the ULCER girl called you Professor, because quote dead Greeks?" Diesel offered him a hand.

"Nah, I just read Greek philosophy for fun. But I used to be a professor of computer engineering and robotics at UNR." Walker pointed at his head. "Dean of Reno Robots." He stood and wiped mud off his ass, "I've got a big, fat Ph.D., and I'm here in the games too, just like you."

"Wow. Did you *fail?*" Diesel walked away from the river.

"My success turned out to be a disaster for those I loved. I failed for all of society, really." His tone dripped with heavy drama. "So, yes. I have failed. Many times. Death would be a welcome change at this point."

A colossal water beast splashed out of the swollen river and roared behind them. Within seconds, it swam to shore. The mutant looked like a hippopotamus but had a long, suckered tentacle for a tail and mane of Medusa-like snakes. The ground trembled as the monster charged at them.

"Do not look at it," Cheng warned.

"Look at what?" Diesel caught a glimpse of the beast. "Is that a cow? From the water?"

"Shut your eyes!" Cheng tapped his temple, and his augmented reality switched into filter mode. His view of the world looked like rainbows as his sunglasses displayed only infrared. The water and trees were cast in blues and greens, while the medusapotamus looked orange and red with white-hot eyes. He drew his ninja knife from the sheath around his waist with his right hand and raised his short ivory staff with the other. The beast howled.

"A medusapotamus." Walker covered his eyes.

(The river cow beast. I have to see it.)

Diesel whispered as she peeked between her fingers. "I thought we didn't name the beasts."

"Well, I just now named it." Walker put his hands over her eyes. "No. Don't look. You'll turn to stone."

"How can Cheng fight something he can't see?"

"Don't you worry about Cheng. You worry about you." Walker put his arm around her head and shielded her face.

Diesel whispered in their huddle cave. "Won't it just attack us?"

"Let's hope Cheng saves our asses."

(Seems like a good time to try my pincer.)

Looking only at her leg, Diesel changed from her tink-tink to the pneumatic lobster claw attachment.

"Don't get any fancy ideas."

"Then what's the point, Walker? I have to fight some time."

"Okay, but do you have to start with a beast?"

On the bank of the Truckee, Cheng stood in a fighting position. He slipped off his half-empty backpack and waved it like a bullfighter's cape, rattling the survival gear inside. Concealing his knife behind the bag with one hand, Cheng twisted the straps around the knobby staff with the other. The medusapotamus stomped its front foot, and the ground shook. Flashing yellowed peg-teeth that jutted from rotten gums, the beast snarled.

Exposed pulp and blood oozed from a broken incisor. Lowering its head, the mutant chomped. A tangled wreath of thirteen cobras around the hippo's face slithered and hissed until the serpents unknotted. The snakes synchronized into a striking pose, then flared their hoods making the hippo's head seem twice as large. The medusapotamus charged.

Diesel twisted the ball joint of her weapon into the harness and locked it tight. She flexed. Nothing happened. She tried again. "Nothing."

(Well that's some shit.)

Walker adjusted Diesel's fitting.

Steady, Cheng held his position on the riverbank. The creature rammed the dangling backpack, and Cheng slashed at its neck before leaping away. His blade missed the throat of the beast, but managed to slice off a cobra head. Cheng spun as the mutant raced past. The cobras remained focused on their passing target as the monster slid deep into muddy slop, stomped through a U-turn, and huffed.

The creature charged again. Cheng crammed his knife into its sheath and anticipated the beast's next move. The medusapotamus opened its jaws wide in a wild act of aggression, and Cheng wedged his short staff across the back of the beast's mouth. The pressure on the mutant's tongue made it gag and bite the staff.

Still running, the creature dragged Cheng. Dangling from the backpack, he managed to swing himself up onto the monster's back. The beast bucked, but Cheng gripped like a cowboy. The cobras hissed and struck, but missed. Shifting his weight forward, Cheng smothered and blocked the snakes with his pack. Then he lassoed the other shoulder strap around the end of the staff sticking out from the edge of the mutant's mouth. He tightened the strap and bridled the beast.

After almost two minutes with Cheng on its back, the medusapotamus stopped fighting and settled down.

"You broke the beast!" Walker cheered.

"Do not look at it!" Cheng yelled.

Walker flinched and hid his face. Then he went back to work on Diesel's rig.

"Cheng did it?"

"He sure did."

Releasing his grip on the backpack handle, Cheng cut off his gray t-shirt with his knife. Avoiding the cobras on each side of the mutants head, Cheng draped the cloth over the monster's eyes and knotted it like a blindfold. Reacting to the restraint, the blind beast curled its tentacle tail around Cheng's waist. It squeezed and lifted the unwelcome rider off its back. Like a slimy, sucker-covered boa constrictor, the tentacle forced the breath out of Cheng until he slipped into unconsciousness.

Diesel vaulted onto the back of the medusapotamus, gripped into the flesh of its rump, and held an impressive handstand. Still upside-down, she arched her back and stretched her hips into a weird, split yoga pose. She aimed her attachment and snipped off the tentacle on her first try.

"With the lobster claw!" She exclaimed.

The creature yelped in pain and lunged forward, tossing Diesel to the ground. She tucked her head into her shoulder and rolled to safety. Cheng landed belly-down on the back of the medusapotamus. If he had any breath left, the fall would have knocked the wind out of him. Then he suddenly gasped. Holding on, Cheng rode the beast until it slowed to a trot. With the tentacle suckers stuck to his bare torso, Cheng crawled into a seated position. He yanked the reins hard to the left and steered the animal back toward his friends.

"Wow! That worked even better than I imagined when I designed it," Walker offered Diesel a hand. "Let me help you to your feet. I mean claw. I mean to your foot *and* claw."

"Thanks, Walker." She wiped mud from her prosthetic leg.

"So how did the clamp action work?"

"Just like you said. I thought about it. I imagined it. I flexed, and it happened."

"It sure did, Diesel." Walker inspected the mechanism.

Cheng rode the blinded and bridled medusapotamus back to his friends. He yanked on the backpack, and the beast came to a halt.

Cheng pointed at the tight tentacle around his stomach. "I could use assistance."

The self-sealing tentacle stopped bleeding on both the animal stump and the severed part wrapped around Cheng. Diesel grabbed the pointy end of the tail, and Walker grabbed the blunt end. The friends pulled in opposite directions to uncoil the freakish appendage. One-by-one, suckers released under pressure, popping and snapping. Diesel worked her way around the butt of the beast while Walker circled the head. A cobra hissed.

"Ouch! Damn!" Walker dropped his end of the severed tail. "It bit me. Shit. I'm bit! I'm *BIT!*"

Diesel gave the rest of the tentacle a good yank to set Cheng free, then dropped the tail. Reacting on instinct, she dashed toward Walker. A Medusa cobra flared and reared, then hissed in her face. Gazing into its glassy black eyes, she backed away without making any more sudden moves.

(You worry about you.)

"Are you all right, Walker?" Diesel asked around the medusapotamus head.

"It burns!" Walker ran away like a spooked animal. He must have sprinted 100 yards before he collapsed to the ground. His body seized and convulsed.

"Cheng?" Diesel poked the back of her stunned friend. "Cheng, *do* something."

Still mounted, Cheng pulled Diesel onto the back of the beast as if it were a horse. She wrapped her arms around Cheng's waist and rode side-saddle. He jerked the backpack reins and dug his heels into the wide ribs of the mutant. The monster reared up in anger, and then submitted. It galloped toward Walker, but soon charged too fast. Cheng yanked the reins again. After three attempts, the beast finally stopped. Diesel and Cheng dismounted, careful to avoid the cobras this time. Diesel dropped to her knee and touched Walker's shoulder.

"What's wrong with him?" She pointed at his foaming mouth.

"Running made his heart beat faster, and that made the poison work faster." Cheng reached into his cargo pocket and pulled out the device. This time, when Cheng depressed the end with his thumb, a thick, long hypodermic needle appeared from the tip of what looked like a jumbo-sized pen. Without speaking or a moment's hesitation, Cheng plunged the needle into Walker's convulsing sternum. The device injected anti-venom directly into Walker's heart. Then the needle retracted automatically, and Cheng shoved the device back into his pocket. Within seconds, Walker sat up, gasping.

"Holy Asgard! Did I just *DIE?*"

"Uh, guys, I have some questions," Diesel said.

The medusapotamus snorted and meandered away toward the edge of the zone. Cheng chased it. "I will answer your questions later, but right now, we have a beast to catch again."

The Union Pacific

June 3, 2037.

Now wearing her running attachment, Diesel rode sideways on the hippo rump and propped Walker against Cheng in front of her.

She stared too long. "We need to find you a shirt, Cheng."

(Find somewhere else to focus. The sunset. There you go. Look at all the pretty colors. Not his naked chest.)

Pink and orange streaks splashed across low clouds. Purpled shadows dipped in mountain canyons.

(Lovely.)

The three friends rode the medusapotamus into the Union Pacific rail yard on the east-side of the zone.

"We should camp here for the night," Cheng said as he pulled the backpack reins to stop the beast. "Walker needs to rest. We all do. We can use a train car for shelter tonight."

Diesel dismounted, then helped Walker slide off the side of the creature. Wobbly but improving, Walker stumbled. Then he almost stood steady. Cheng jumped down and retrieved the severed tentacle draped around the neck of the beast. Rigor mortis had set in during their journey, so the detached tail held its horseshoe shape. Cheng tossed the dead appendage into an open boxcar.

Walker shuffled over to examine the tentacle. "Why are we keeping this?"

"It is protein. It will nourish us."

Walker poked a slimy sucker and made a yucky face.

Picking at the tentacle, Diesel objected. "Eat that? No thank you."

"When was the last time you ate, Diesel?" Cheng twisted the backpack strap around the boxcar's door handle. Then he searched the area.

"I had some dandelions and a handful of wild goji berries this morning."

"That is not enough to sustain energy. Are you not hungry?" Cheng found a length of rusty chain. He tossed it into a dented shopping cart that was missing one of its wheels.

"Of course I'm hungry."

Cheng forced the cart across the rock and rails, using it to gather scraps of wood. Diesel studied the blinded medusapotamus head as it swayed toward her.

(It's listening to me.)

The snakes in its mane wove around each other to conserve heat as the serpents rested.

"Hey, Walker, do snakes sleep?" She helped him hop onto the edge of the boxcar.

"Of course snakes sleep."

A few cars away, Cheng rummaged through garbage. After a few minutes of exploration, he crammed the stiff and resistant wheels of the half-full cart through the gravel. Once he returned to the boxcar, Cheng busted up a pallet for firewood. He stacked the splintered lumber into a teepee and went back to scavenging.

"You smoke, Cheng. Do you have your lighter?"

Cheng reached into his pocket, pulled out his Zippo, and tossed it to her. Diesel flipped it open and struck the wheel. She held the blue and gold flame to the wood for the longest time.

"It didn't ignite. Only left this scorch mark." Diesel pointed at the blackness.

"We need some tinder." Walker gestured to a sun-faded and torn piece of cardboard box from his perch. "Can you grab that?"

Diesel fetched the cardboard and tore it into strips. Then she wedged them between the pieces of wood. Fixated on the beast instead of her chore, she asked, "So why can we look at it now?"

"Because its eyes are covered. If you look into its eyes, you'll turn to stone," Walker answered.

Diesel lit the cardboard and shoved a flaming end into the center of their scrap pyramid. The reluctant wood smoldered. Then it burned. "That's just weird. I have a hard time believing that whole 'turn to stone' story."

"Well, let's just say, that's one theory I don't need to test. I've seen it happen first hand." Walker rubbed the pair of grotesquely swollen fang marks on the meat between his thumb and palm. "I ought to clean and dress this. I don't want it to get infected." He spit at the animal in disgust, "Filthy beast."

Cheng returned with a three-quarter tread of a blown out semi-truck tire and a rusty piece of sheetmetal. He dropped the loot and kicked a loose board off the rickety pallet. Once he freed a splintered plank he used it to pound the metal into shape using the edge of the boxcar as an anvil.

"So, Cheng, I have questions," Diesel said. "First, why did you say Bull's a bad guy? Second, how come you can look at the medusapotamus without turning into stone? Third, what was that thing you stabbed Walker in the heart with? Fourth—"

"You should just forget about Bull," Cheng snipped as he slung the radial tire tread around the beast's neck covering the sleeping cobras. He fussed and got it into place just right. Then, proud of his work, he smiled at his friends. "I made a snake guard."

Walker nodded. "May I field some of these questions, Cheng?"

"That would be excellent." Cheng laid the remaining shopping cart contents in a line on the edge of the boxcar next to Walker. Then he flipped the basket upside down over the fire. Using a piece of bent rebar, he banged on the bottom.

"So, it's okay if I tell her. *Everything?*" Walker asked.

Dirt and rust trickled down into the fire. "Yes, It is okay."

"You see, Cheng and I have known each other for—" Walker nudged Cheng with his foot. "How long has it been now?"

Cheng sorted through his new-found supplies. "We met a year, five months, and two weeks ago." He swatted at Walker's foot. Then he slung the medusapotamus tail onto the shopping cart grill. It sizzled.

"Yeah. That's right. Two Christmases ago." Walker nodded.

Cheng concentrated on fitting the hammered metal over the head of the mutant. He rested it on the temporary t-shirt blinder and eyed it for size. Then he snatched the metal and started pounding it against the boxcar again. After a few rounds of hammering and turning, Cheng fitted the blinding mask onto the beast.

"Christmas?" Diesel asked. "I had a Christmas once."

"Once?" Walker did a double take. "I guess that makes sense. *They* aren't exactly the festive type."

"Actually." Diesel counted on her fingers while doing math in her head. "I've had seven Christmases thanks to my friend, Ernesta."

(I sure miss her.)

"Well, look at you. That must have been a big deal for a ward." Impressed, he watched juices bubble up and roast out of the tentacle before dripping into the fire.

"Ernesta always brought me a gift of deluxe art supplies at Christmas. Just in time too, I'd run out of paint every November. I love to paint. I wish I had a sketch pad and some pastels right now. I could've captured this magnificent sunset."

"I have seen her work. She is quite the artist." Cheng took his eyes off his task of fastening the mask to the beast to smile at her. One of the cobras hissed and struck at him. With lightning quick reflexes, Cheng snatched his hand away. He smirked at her again and winked. "Do not worry. It missed. I am not bit."

(Damn. He's charming.)

"Why don't you just kill that thing?" Diesel asked.

"What good would killing it do? I have better plans."

"Oh, yeah? What's that?" Walker asked.

"I am going to weaponize this beast," Cheng said, yanking his carved staff out of the mouth of the medusapotamus. He unwound his backpack from the stick, and tossed it at Walker. Then Cheng twisted the tip of his tactical knife to drill a hole in each end of the ivory stick. He pounded the end of the chain against the boxcar until the links opened enough for him to force each one through the staff.

"Yeah, Cheng helped build your leg. He's handy. A real inventor. I don't think we could have done it without him."

"I wondered about that. You guys sure made this rig fast." Diesel showed off her prosthetic by hopping on it.

Cheng turned to explain, "We had been work—"

Walker blurted, "Cheng's an *ALIEN!*"

Diesel shoved Walker's shoulder hard, "Get *OUT!*"

"No. He is!"

"No way." Diesel stared at Cheng waiting for a response.

Cheng stopped working long enough to look at Diesel. "I am alien." Uncomfortable, he looked away and went back to work without further explanation.

"Cheng's sunglasses are a rare technology. An alien technology…"

She looked at Cheng. "He looks like a regular person to me."

"Yes. He does. That's the brilliance of it. His kind can morph and assume the form of the dominant species on any inhabited planet. It's his special skill."

"Come on. You guys are messing with me," Diesel stepped closer to Cheng. Looking for a flaw or anything that might tip her off, she surveyed him up and down lingering a bit too long on his bare, muscular chest as he worked.

(That's too much. Hot. I can't take it.)

"He's just a normal guy," she said.

Cheng walked to the box car, and Diesel followed him, still staring. He unzipped his backpack. "I am not from Earth, Diesel. My origin is a planet called, well the closest way to pronounce it in English is 'Theta Rhonda Four.'"

"Why did you come here?"

"Our planet died. An asteroid impact caused an ice age. Some of my species survived for many generations after the disaster, but most of my kind died before we could escape. It is a complicated story best reserved for another time."

"That means you don't want to tell me." Diesel looked disappointed.

"No, it just means that now is not the time." Cheng pulled a flask out of his backpack.

Walker snatched the liquor from his friend, "You brought the Tullamore Dew." He unscrewed the metal cap and took a big swig. Then another.

Perplexed, Diesel asked, "Tell her more due?"

"Irish whiskey," Walker said. "But none for you. You're too young."

"Right. Too young to drink and too young to gamble, but plenty old enough to die in the games. I get it," Diesel sulked.

Following the train tracks, she looked westward. "Why don't we just ride the train into California and get out of here?"

"Never!" Belligerent, Walker shouted.

"What is the harm?" Cheng gestured for Walker to share the alcohol.

"No way. She's my daughter's age." Still drinking, Walker sat with his legs dangling over the edge of the box car.

(He had a daughter? I never thought of Walker as a dad.)

"I thought your daughter was deceased."

Walker chugged more whiskey. "I mean, if my daughter were still alive, she'd be almost the same age as Diesel."

"It may be nighttime, but that does not mean there will not be more fighting. Maybe you should slow down and keep your wits."

"Wits are the last thing I need. My little girl's dead. I already escaped death once today. Screw it."

Changing the topic, Cheng addressed Diesel instead, "The Union Pacific still runs all the way to the California coast, but visitors need a travel Visa to cross into the country of Pacifica." Cheng rubbed the scar on the back of his hand. "And players are not permitted to have Visas."

"What if we stowed away?"

"Duh, collars." Walker yanked on his. "Damn it. Just stay off the trains. Why doesn't anyone listen to me?"

"Shut up, drunky," Diesel joked.

"The intoxicated man has a point. Regardless of whether we ride a train or not, our compliance collars would detonate if we crossed the perimeter of the zone. We would not even get close to California."

"Listen. I'm telling you, even if it were possible, California is not the answer. And trains are never the answer." Walker struggled to suppress his drunkenness to sound reasonable. "The United States built the wall to keep us undesirables out. But no one wants to go to America anyway. That place is a hot mess. Nevadaland is the place to be. Mountain borders in the east and west keep us safe from nuclear fall out. Rain shadows also make good fallout shadows. We just have to escape from Reno. We really gotta get outa Reno. The wilds would be better." His argument broke down into paranoid ramblings. "*They* run this city. *They* will never let me be. *They* hate me. I used to be a God. Now I am their slave. But outside Reno, in the wilds, I might have a chance. I could go total gray rock and disappear. Nevada. Battle born ready, bitches." Walker collapsed.

"Okay, then what about heading east?" Diesel's gaze followed the tracks in the opposite direction. "Trains go two ways. There's more Nevadaland that way."

"We tried that at the river," Cheng said.

"*NO* trains! Don't you listen? There's no way out on a train," Walker mumbled and slurred. "*They* win. *They* always win."

"Would you like to see my glasses?" Changing topics again, Cheng removed his shades and offered Diesel a distraction.

Still studying Cheng for any hint of alien, Diesel took his sunglasses. "Your eyes are green like mine."

(I never really got a good look before. Damn. He's handsome.)

Without speaking, Cheng turned away and finished constructing the stronger, more stable, bridle for the medusapotamus. Diesel fiddled with his glasses. Aside from a male

56

USB port on one of the temples, the technology looked just like a pair of sporty shades. She tried the sunglasses on.

(Nothing. I can't see a thing. It's too dark out here.)

"How do you see with these things at night?"

"Cannot understand well." Cheng approached her.

Squiggly lines showed up on the inside of the lenses. Diesel squinted and flinched away.

"Translated?"

"I guess. Is that your language?" Diesel read a fresh set of green squiggles.

Still holding his carved staff, Cheng pulled a tuft of hair back from his temple, exposing a female port that sunk deep into his skull just above his ear.

"Whoa."

"I'll drink to that." Walker finished off the whiskey.

"Plug in head." He pointed at the port.

More squiggles flashed as Diesel gave the glasses back to Cheng. He slid on his shades and docked the technology in the ear port. The connection flashed a little blue light and then went dark.

"What's the port for?"

"Biochemical energy powers this technology. The port keeps the glasses charged and offers auxiliary functions. Battery power expires after about an hour. This technology translates, shows alternate views, searches for data, and offers many other functions. There is a little button here." He touched his temple. "Here." He touched the bridge of his nose. "And here." He touched his other temple. "The lenses are cameras. These also have rearview cameras at the back of each arm of the frame." He touched the back tips. "But the augmented reality will not work for you because you do not have a port."

"How do I get one?"

"It has to be installed surgically."

(Surgery? No thanks. Last time. They took my girlie organs. Because I bled. THEY didn't like that I bled.)

"No thanks. I'm a bit phobic when it comes to doctors. I'm terrified of surgery." Diesel took a good look at Cheng's carved stick. "That doesn't look like wood."

"It is not wood."

"What is it?"

Cheng hesitated.

(He doesn't want to tell me. Why not? Wait a minute. You know what that looks like? No. It's not. It can't be.)

Drunk, Walker roused and sang the old spiritual, "The shin bone's connected to the knee bone. Dem bones, dem bones, dem dry bones." Walker slurred and fell backward again. Laying back, he stared at the rusty roof of the boxcar with his legs hanging limply over the side. "Dem bones, dem bones, dem dry bones."

Diesel took two steps back. "Oh my *GOD*. Is that. Is that my *LEG?*"

"We could not just throw it away like trash."

"Really? So what happened to the *rest* of it?"

The silence between friends lasted an eternity.

"Cheng, what happened to the rest of my leg? What happened to the skin, and the blood, and the muscle—"

"I ate it!" Walker blurted. His words echoed through the boxcar and back into his face. Walker swatted at the sound bouncing around his head.

"You what?" Diesel bent over, breathless.

(I'm going to puke.)

"Diesel?" Cheng touched her shoulder.

"Don't touch me!" Diesel shrank away from Cheng. "He's intoxicated, right?. Tell me he's just drunk. Tell me it's not true."

Walker pushed himself up, but his legs still hung like curing sausages. "I'm sorry, Diesel. I'm sorry I ate your leg."

The smell of the roasting medusapotamus tail hit her nostrils.

(Stings like when Bull punched me in the nose.)

Diesel vomited on the railroad tracks.

"You should have let him die." She scowled at Cheng.

"I agree," Walker said, as he propped himself up to sit. "You *should* have let me die."

"Walker, please do not—" Cheng said.

"I couldn't help myself, Diesel. I don't blame you for hating me. I know I've got a problem. It's like an addiction. I try not to ever eat people anymore, but sometimes I slip. Your leg. It was just sitting there, and it looked so tasty. And after a couple days in the deep freezer, I couldn't help myself. And once I had a taste. I ate the whole damn thing. I ate it frozen. I have a sickness, Diesel. I hate myself. I'm so sorry. Please forgive me."

In the boxcar, the bloody bride appeared on her knees behind Walker. Amelia kissed his cheek and held an elegant silver knife to his throat. "Let's put this poor fella outta his misery." She smiled at Diesel. "You want me to kill 'em for you?"

"No," Diesel said to her.

"I don't blame you," Walker said. "I can't forgive myself either."

"Dammit! Shut up!" Diesel screamed back at him. "Just stop talking."

"Yes, get angry," Amelia said. "You have the right to be angry. I mean, hell. He *ATE* you! You should be enraged."

Diesel flexed her Wolverine claw-gloved left hand and clenched her right fist. She took a step forward.

(I almost forgot about this weapon.)

Cheng shoved his finished bridle into the mouth of the medusapotamus. He slid the attached metal hood over the animal's face, pulled his shirt from underneath, and slipped it on like a vest. Meanwhile, Walker swung his feet back and forth like a kid sitting on the edge of a dock gazing into a lake.

"I mean you're even better now than you were before, right?" Walker gestured at her mechanical leg. "So it was worth taking the chance."

"Please, stop talking, Walker." Cheng poked the fire and turned the roasting tentacle with his bent rebar.

"What's that supposed to mean?" Diesel asked, and Walker looked away. "Wait. You *knew?*"

The silence of both her friends answered her question. "You *KNEW* the halo would blow!" Diesel kicked a rock with her tink-tink foot as she shouted. "Fuck you, Walker."

"You said the offensive word."

"No more from you, Alien Guy! What *are* you, the dictionary police? You shut up. You just shut up! Walker *ATE* my *leg*. If there's ever an appropriate time to use the word 'fuck,' it's when you just found out that your friend detonated a device that severed your leg and then later snacked on your frozen ankle." Diesel yanked on her blue collar. "Besides, I'm an adult now. I can use *ALL* the words, not just the ones from *the book!*"

"Girls are not supposed to curse," Cheng said.

"Didn't I ask you to shut up? Now I can say *ALL* the things I hear in my head. Even the dark things. I like sunshine and hope. It's like the color yellow. But not everything is optimistic and proper all the time. Not everything is yellow. This is *NOT* a yellow moment!"

"It's vulgar," Walker slurred.

Diesel turned toward her cannibal friend in a deliberate and dramatic manner, "Me? I'm vulgar? Because I'm a girl and I dared to use a word reserved for men?" Diesel lifted her tink-tink knee-high. "You *ATE* my leg, Walker! That was *ME.* You consumed me. It doesn't get any more vulgar than that."

"I can't argue with that," Walker mumbled.

Amelia put her hand to her ear like she was listening closely. She knelt beside Walker.

"I'm *NOT* a *girl* anymore. I've graduated. I'm an adult. I'm here—a *player* just like you guys. I've got just as much to lose as any man. So, stop treating me like a child. I can't believe *you ATE MY LEG*, and now your inebriated ass is telling me what words I can and cannot use? I don't think so, Mister Cannibal Man!"

As if on cue, the bloody bride slit Walker's throat, but he still sat there like a drunk idiot. Amelia smiled as blood sprayed from his severed jugular. Then Diesel smiled too. And then Walker spoke and ruined the women's shared bloody fantasy.

"I wasn't sure the halo was safe. I only worried that it *might* blow. I knew there was a chance. Just a chance, that it could. We had the bionic leg ready just in case things went wrong—"

"You *PLANNED* this? You conspirator!" Diesel screamed as she lunged toward him. She punched Walker hard in the nose, and he fell back and hit his head. "You stole my choice."

Walker touched his throbbing nose and pondered the blood on his hand. "I deserve that."

"I *HATE* you," Diesel hissed as she climbed onto Walker and kept pounding him with punches. "Who do you think you are?" She slashed his cheek open with her claw-glove.

(I like seeing HIS blood.)

Elegant, the bloody bride danced like a ballerina inside the boxcar. She spun on her tiptoes as Cheng jumped into the car and pulled Diesel off Walker. He tried to restrain his angry friend, but she wiggled and twisted out of his grasp. After breaking free, she scrambled to the corner. Amelia pranced over to her, and together, the indignant women glared at the men. The ghost and three friends struggled with an endless stalemate.

Then Diesel's old roommate, Wyatt, sneaked from between two train cars. In a moment, he stabbed the grilled tentacle with his spear and swiped their dinner. He dashed away.

"Dammit. What's *wrong* with people?" Full of rage, Diesel chased after Wyatt, all alone, into the night.

The Spaghetti Bowl

Tonight.

Chasing the thief across crumbling surface streets toward the interstate highway, Diesel shouted into the darkness, "Give it back, Wyatt!"

"Never," He taunted, as he scampered up the trafficless on-ramp and past a hitchhiking reg'. Enjoying the game, he led her to the major interstate exchange known as the Spaghetti Bowl.

As the players passed, a dirty hitchhiker raised his arms wide overhead and clapped. "Are you all ready?" The homeless hippy reg' bounced and swayed like a choir director in a southern baptist church. "Right here y'all. I said, 'Are you all ready?' Put your hands together," he chanted in time with his claps at an imaginary audience down the ramp.

The grilled medusapotamus tail bounced on the end of Wyatt's spear as he jogged between two empty lanes. A yellow-collar dressed as a prostitute, or maybe a rockstar groupie, danced suggestively on the concrete foundation of a missing streetlamp. She whipped her ratty blonde wig, by tossing her head side-to-side. Wyatt paused as she spread her legs, bent over, and shook her money maker. He wished she still had the lamp-pole. Diesel missed the point.

(There's no music.)

"Do *NOT* piss me off, Wyatt." Close behind, Diesel chased without having to run full speed. Their sham pursuit barely increased her heart rate. It wasn't serious, yet. "Come on, Wyatt. I just found out that one of my best friends ate my leg tonight. So, I don't know. Maybe cut me a break and give back my dinner. Maybe this once, don't be a dick."

Wyatt froze. He spun around to address Diesel, and she nearly ran into him. "Wait? What? Someone ate your leg tonight?"

Diesel grabbed at the tentacle and tore it from his javelin. "No. I just found out tonight. He ate my leg a while ago but just told me now. You know I lost my leg weeks ago. Now gimme this. Give it!"

Wyatt yanked on the opposite end of the roasted beast and started a half-serious, yet full-bizarre, monster meat tug-of-war. "Who was it? Was it Bull? That guy looks like he'd love to eat someone."

"No, not Bull. It was Walker."

"No way," Wyatt swept Diesel's legs with a low spinning roundhouse kick, knocking her on her ass. While she tumbled, he snatched the grilled tail and ran further up the ramp.

"Wyatt! You bastard." Diesel scrambled to her feet.

(Well, to my one REAL foot and the tink-tink.)

She chased after him again—right into an ambush. A dozen drones flew toward Diesel and hovered high above her.

(Shit. Something's up.)

From all directions, each drone pointed a spotlight at her. Diesel threw her hands over her eyes to adjust to the light. Hiding from the drones, Wyatt stopped in the shadows. He tried to provoke her by flapping the now cold, but still cooked, beast tentacle at her. The gesture seemed desperate and pointless. Wyatt's blue collar flashed white, but Diesel didn't notice, because she couldn't see with the bright lights in her eyes. Instead of playing tag with him, she scanned the intersection of ramps and three-lane highways looking for danger.

(Nothing. I'm dead center. But something's out there. I can feel it.)

Down ramp, a red rooster comb bobbed over the horizon. Floppy orange feet schlepped and scuffed on the road. A plume of yellow feathers and cartoon eyes appeared in the distance. Before she spotted the beak, she knew.

(It's Chickenman.)

He scowled through the face-hole under his yellow plastic beak. Wielding a sledgehammer high overhead, his foam chicken feet hindered his intensity, leaving a comical impression. His orange collar flashed white, like he was being paged.

(Or paging someone.)

Diesel dropped back into a wide fighting stance. The theme from the classic boxing movie, *Rocky,* blasted out of the circling drones' speakers. The streetlights illuminated. Then all at once, regs' climbed over the concrete highway barriers. In a matter of seconds, a cheering audience surrounded the multi-spoked highway interchange.

(He's going to kill me.)

The bloody bride appeared among the faces in the crowd. Chickenman continued his awkward, and painfully slow, jogging approach with a hundred yards to go before he would be any threat.

The ghost smiled at her friend. "He's not even a player, Diesel."

"Then why the sledgehammer?"

The eager crowd closed the gap, and Diesel lost sight of the menacing chicken man.

"*They* want a show. It's all a show." Amelia winked at her.

(To hell with it. Who cares anymore? Give 'em what THEY want.)

As the *Rocky* theme faded out, Diesel held her arms out at her sides and spun in a circle like an old-school Wonder Woman. Then without music, she gyrated some kind of sexy dance that came off more embarrassing than alluring. As if on cue, drones blasted a weird burlesque pop-synth song to accompany and encourage her performance. Diesel wiggled her hips and shook her unharnessed boobs.

The reg' dressed as a prostitute complained from further down the ramp, "Hey, that's my job!" Without an audience, she jumped up and down on her concrete pedestal and shouted, "Players aren't supposed to be dancers. Hey! I'm doing the sexy." She squatted and bounced while trying to get the attention of the spectators again. "Hey, look at me. I'm the sexy one. Over here."

The dancer's collar turned red-hot and vibrated. She heeded her warning, dropped her protest, sat down, and shut up. The audience gathered around Diesel so tight that the chicken man couldn't get through with his sledgehammer. He became just another face in the crowd.

"Watch this, suckers!" Diesel flipped into a double cartwheel.

The mob "oohed" and "ahed." On her next turn, she held a handstand. She wagged and pointed her fake leg at the audience. Shifting her weight onto one arm, she twisted the lock to her prosthetic and removed the runner's attachment with her free hand. Like a yoga contortionist, she holstered her tink-tink and selected the circular saw from her leather back-sling. In a second, she plugged the saw-leg into its harness socket and locked it into place.

When she stuck her landing, she flexed her right thigh, and the saw blade spun, kicking sparks on the macadam and smoky exhaust into the air. The crowd cheered.

"I am Diesel Duran." She wiggled her ass and made the crowd go wild. "Let's rumble!"

The mob roared.

"Wyatt!" Diesel yelled at the drones like a hamming professional wrestler. "Bring me Wyatt."

Flying cameras circled over the crowd until one spotted her former roommate. Two more joined to zoom on her adversary. Wyatt dropped the medusapotamus bait at his side and touched the tip of his spear, pretending it felt super sharp. Overacting, his performance came off cartoonish. The people parted to open a path to Diesel as the drones herded Wyatt toward her. His collar flashed white.

(What? Did I just page him? Did that work because the drones are broadcasting? Or because I'm the center of attention? Probably both. Nice.)

The music stopped, and instead, three words broadcasted on repeat through speakers, "Fight for it. Fight for it. Fight for it."

Soon all the regs' in the crowd chanted, "Fight for it. Fight for it."

Knowing what would happen next, Wyatt and Diesel locked eyes. She stretched and flexed the fingers of her left hand. Her claw-glove responded.

(Satisfying.)

Wyatt twirled the long staff of his spear like a black-belt entering the ring in his dojo. Diesel lifted her saw-leg to the side in an impressive stretch and spun on her toe like Jean-Claude Van Damme in *Street Fighter*. Holding her balance, she twitched her right quad. Her circular saw revved three times. The mob roared with approval.

(I've had just about enough of this shit. This douchebag. This whole damn day.)

Stepping left then right, like a football player running through tires, Wyatt charged. He stabbed his javelin at her. Diesel misjudged his next move and stepped into his punch. His fist landed square on her nose. Pinpoints of light circled her vision. It stung. Tears rushed into her eyes.

(NO. No time for crying. This is REAL.)

Stumbling back, Diesel shook off the sharp pain. A reg' old enough to be her grandfather stepped out from the crowd and helped himself to a handful of her ass. Squealing like a woman goosed by her boss at the company Christmas party, Diesel lurched forward.

(Opportunist!)

The creeper reg' chortled, as Wyatt spun and attacked Diesel again. White knuckled, Wyatt raised his spear high and lunged at her. Stepping out and turning her foot 90 degrees, Diesel flexed her harnessed thigh. Her circular blade dug into the asphalt, yanking her hard to the left. The saw-wheel spun her around and drove her behind the reg'. Diesel relaxed, and the power tool stopped. She choked the old man with her forearm and ducked behind him.

(Be useful. Be my shield.)

Wyatt's spear descended at full speed, just narrowly missing Diesel's forearm while piercing the scuzzball in the throat. Momentum forced it through the regs' wrinkled neck. Behind him, the tip of the javelin scratched Diesel's cheek. She flinched away and released the body.

(Handy. Thanks old man.)

The creeper dropped like a sack of potatoes, taking Wyatt's spear to the ground with him. For the first time, Diesel got close enough to fight with her claw. She hit Wyatt in the jaw with a back-fist, then raked his face. His cheek split open in three places. Wyatt reeled from the pain and gushed blood.

(YES!)

"Payback's a bitch," Amelia cheered.

Diesel yanked on the spear stuck in the dying geezer's gullet. She planted the sole of her boot over his eyes as he gurgled on blood. She heaved with all she had, but the javelin wouldn't budge. Then his orange collar went dark. Diesel stepped off his face, revved her saw-leg, and chopped the javelin shaft, leaving only an inch of nub sticking out from the throat.

(Wyatt'll never be able to get a grip on that.)

Diesel took the long wooden handle. "And now I have a long staff," She proclaimed.

The crowd applauded. Wyatt tackled her from behind. The side of Diesel's forehead hit the ground and the rod fell out of her hand. The stick rolled into the mob, as the spot right above her eyebrow cracked open and gushed.

"Hmpf. Wha? Damn."

At first her wound stung, then it got numb and sticky. Wyatt jumped onto her back, splattering his blood all over her. Straddling her back-holster, Wyatt crammed his knee into the soft spot under her shoulder blade. Stunned, Diesel wiggled, but couldn't get any leverage. Then Wyatt punched her in the back of the head. Her face hit the pavement.

Looking for an exit, she lifted her head. He punched her, and her face hit the ground again.

(Shit.)

He did it again, and again.

Amelia coached her, "Stay down. Stop taking double whiplash hits."

With her saw-leg spinning through the air, Diesel fluttered her legs in desperation, but she couldn't reach Wyatt.

He laughed at her attempt, "You smell like a pathetic chainsaw."

(Do something. He'll kill you.)

Diesel tried a push-up, but Wyatt jabbed his knee deeper into her shoulder, and she just collapsed. Then something hard poked the middle of her back. Through the leather of her holster, between her tink-tink and lobster claw, Wyatt jabbed Diesel with the first erection she ever felt. At the same time, he bashed the back of her head over and over. His rage boner added insult to injury as her brain swam and her responses delayed.

(This is it. My first real fight, and I'm gonna die.)

Her eyelids fluttered as she danced on the edge of consciousness. Amelia glided through the frenzied crowd. The bloody bride knelt down on all fours next to Diesel and smiled.

(Why are you so happy?)

Tiring, Wyatt took a break between blows, and the ghost bride kissed Diesel on the corner of her mouth.

"Don't worry, love. It's almost over," Amelia whispered.

Diesel shut her eyes and embraced the blackness. A drone swooped in for the extreme-close-up of her death. The crowd inched in closer and quieted to listen. Diesel went limp.

"Last words?" a robotic voice prompted from the drone.

Out of nowhere, Chickenman appeared and buried his sledgehammer in the side of Wyatt's skull. In a split second,

Wyatt's face went from rage to shock and froze as his skull collapsed under pressure. His body succumbed to impact momentum as he fell off Diesel.

Amelia screamed in her friend's ear, "Diesel? Wake up, Diesel. Come on; you're not dead. *WAKE* up. *GET UP!*"

Groggy, Diesel raised her head. Pain surged down her spine, and she dropped again.

"Diesel, enough! This way. Come on. You can do it. Flip over. *NOW!*" Like a video game assist, the ghost bride coached Diesel to roll over in her direction. She smacked both her palms on the ground. "Here's your next move. Don't think. *DO.*"

Diesel rolled onto her back.

"Remember that back roll flip?" Amelia waved both hands back and forth from toe to head over Diesel, then screamed, "Do it. Do *IT NOW.*"

Diesel nodded and summoned all the energy she could. Raising her hands over her head, she planted her palms on the road and pulled her knees into her chest. Her whole body relaxed then tensed as she flung herself into a backflipping handstand. Her saw-leg whirled through the air just as the Chickenman dove for his sledgehammer.

As her feet flipped over her head, Diesel's circular saw cut deep into the chicken man's torso. Yellow feathers flew through the air followed by blood splatter and then by chunky organ bits. His blood showered her. By the time Diesel stuck the landing, chicken man had been eviscerated and she was drenched. Unlike the others, his death took longer. He stumbled like a zombie grasping at his dangling entrails. Trying to collect and shove his guts back inside his gaping abdomen, the assless chicken man looked like a drunken gore juggler. High on blood lust, the crowd screamed and surged like an organism. Dizzy, Diesel couldn't believe her eyes. She gaped at the carnage she had caused.

(What IS that? I always thought he was a black man.)

The front of chicken man's costume fell around his knees. Where skin should have been, Chickenman had blood-drenched feathers instead. Despite all the gore, some of his feathers were a beautiful dark-brown like a Cuban rooster.

(That doesn't make sense. I have a concussion.)

The crowd wanted more brutality, but Diesel inspected the dying street dealer instead.

(Chicken man is—was—a literal chickenman. A mutant. Only his face and ass look human. The parts he exposed. He wanted everyone to think he was human. Almost normal, just a weirdo. I guess it's better to let people believe that you're a fetish freak than to let them know you've become something, NOT human.)

Diesel peeked into his hood, and instead of hair, he had a red rubberlike comb. A red dangling rooster neck had been tucked deep behind his mask. Under his foam feet, he had lizard-like talons with long claws. She peeled off his nitrile gloves, and underneath, his scaly dinosaur hands matched his feet.

The crowd started chanting again, "Fight for it. Fight for it. Fight for it."

(Cut me a break, people.)

The regs' pushed and slammed into each other like a rowdy mosh pit.

(It's never enough. It will never be enough.)

73

Someone grabbed her arm and yanked her into the mob. A drone buzzed by her ear to catch all the action. On the fringes of the crowd, money exchanged as Diesel was declared the winner.

Annoyed and amped up on her first-ever taste of adrenalin, she snagged the quadcopter drone. It whirled and tugged to get away, but she didn't let it. Instead, she pulled it closer and shoved her face in the camera.

"You want more? You'll get more. Remember my name." Then, in an uncharacteristic rage, Diesel whipped out her left tit and crammed it into the camera. "*DIESEL*. My name is Diesel. And *YOU LOVE* me!" Disgusted, she shoved her boob back into her tank top and tossed the drone away.

It almost crashed into the ground, but recovered and flew to safety like a dog with its tail between its legs. The reg' crowd hoisted Diesel up onto many shoulders. Dozens of hands supported her back as she surfed over a sea of spectators. She wasn't used to being touched, let alone having all those hands on her at once.

(Stay relaxed. Stay relaxed, or you'll wind up sawing someone's head off.)

The mob cheered, "Diesel, Diesel, Diesel," as it roamed down the ramp and carried her away in victory.

A swarm of drones followed the pack of people broadcasting all the footage for home viewers. Back at the abandoned battle scene, three men lay dead. The street lights went dark. Pee-do Grandpa piled into a sad lump with a truncated spear crammed into his throat. Forgotten Wyatt who started it all, splayed out like roadkill with his skull crushed. And the Assless Chickenman, a bisected Big Bird held together by his spine, soaked in a puddle of yellow feathers. No one mourned these fallen.

Except for one man—one man stood enraged in the shadows. Despondent and furious, he emerged and knelt over Chickenman and swore he'd get revenge. Angel Rodriguez made one last vow to his best friend, "I will kill that bitch for this."

The Harvest

Soon Later.

Cheng and Walker rode toward the deserted Spaghetti Bowl on the medusapotamus. An evening breeze blew trash and tumbleweeds into a mini-cyclone nearby. Walker pointed at a drainage ditch near the on-ramp.

"Cheng, look."

"What is it?"

"I saw something move down there."

Jerking on the chain and approaching with caution, Cheng directed the lumbering mutant toward the gutter. Disoriented, a blood-covered Diesel writhed on the ground with leaves and trash matted in her short hair. Cheng handed the reins to Walker, then jumped down to help her.

"Diesel?" He touched her shoulder. "There is so much blood. Are you all right?"

Mumbling, she rolled. "Cheng?"

"Can you stand?" He helped her up. "What happened to you?"

"I won."

"You don't look like a winner."

"You shut up, Walker," Diesel snapped.

"She's fine," Walker said on high from beastback. "Hard to look at, but fine."

Cheng helped Diesel out of the trench. "She is beaten and bleeding."

Her saw-leg slipped on the loose gravel, and after stumbling twice, she paused to balance on her good leg. Switching out of fight mode, she changed attachments and locked on her tink-tink. Then she scrambled up the steep grade. "Another fight broke out, and the drones took off to cover it." Diesel pointed off the highway. "That way. Everyone went that way." Her head throbbed, and she doubled over. "Those bastards dumped me for the next fight. Just threw me in the gutter like trash."

"Aw, shit," Walker laughed, still drunk. "You got ditched."

Diesel shot him a nasty look, emphasized by her headache. "Shut your cannibal mouth."

"You said you won. Did you fight?" Cheng asked.

"I did." Aching, Diesel straightened up. "Up there. I killed Wyatt." She paused. "And others."

"Did you retrieve our dinner?" Cheng asked.

(*I cannot believe you just asked me that.*)

"I was busy."

"So, the tail is gone?"

"Yes. The tail is gone, Cheng. Thanks for caring." Diesel scrubbed blood from her face with the bottom of her shirt.

"I do care. I asked if you were all right first."

"Drop it, Cheng, or you'll wind up in the dog house with me."

"My claw-glove's gone too." Diesel held out her bare hand and wiggled her stiff fingers. "Someone swiped it." She stretched and cracked her bruised knuckles. "Both of you, drop it." Despite her headache, Diesel sprinted up the ramp, "Come on. I want to show you guys something."

Cheng ran after her.

Walker struggled to get the medusapotamus to follow his commands. He crammed his heels in the creature's fat ribs and flicked the chains. "Go."

It growled and stomped its front foot.

"Go, critter." Walker scooted his hips forward, trying to encourage the animal. He shook the chains, but only managed to wake the snakes under the blown out tire-guard. They hissed

At the top of the ramp, Diesel spotted two men driving a dilapidated airport ATV. The dented and rusty Polaris towed a jury-rigged flatbed trailer made of a truck axel and planks of bloodstained wood. She turned to Cheng with her finger over her lips.

"Shhhhh."

Cheng crept up next to her, and the two friends ducked behind a concrete barrier. Walker trudged up the ramp pulling the reluctant beast's chain. Eventually, he made it to his friends, and the players managed to hide with the medusapotamus.

"'Vesters," Walker whispered.

"Walker, your breath." Diesel covered her nose and turned away.

"It smells like a dog's ass, doesn't it?" Walker sniffed himself.

"A drunk dog's ass, yes."

"These are the harvesters?" Cheng asked.

"Yes. Here for the dead bodies," Walker said. "We should go." He went back down the ramp.

"We just got here, Walker," Diesel shout-whispered at him. "Get back here."

For once, Walker obeyed. "Look, 'vesters have a dirty job, and we shouldn't be here. *They* take the deceased to the hospital morgue for—" He stopped himself from finishing his sentence.

The harvesters wore black breathable rubberized suits, thick red rubber gloves, red rain boots, and respirators. The men worked together to lift and toss the corpses onto the trailer. First Grandpa, and then Wyatt plopped on board. Then the bottom half of Chickenman broke away when the 'vesters tried to lift him.

"Whoa, you killed the chicken man?" Walker asked.

"It was an accident."

The 'vesters tossed the top of Chickenman onto the trailer, and went back for the second piece, but left his guts on the ground. The harvesters left the weapons behind too. Without wasting a second, the workers hopped into the four-wheeler and drove southwest.

"Let's follow." Diesel jumped on the back of the medusapotamus and sat sideways. "Come on, Cheng. Take me to the hospital."

79

Cheng climbed onto the beast and sat behind her. "You should drive. Do you sit like that because—"

"Because I can't grip the beast with the tink-tink. The more I try to hold on with my legs, the more my harness slips." She adjusted the belt around her thigh.

"That is what I thought."

Walker hesitated. "This is a bad idea."

"We could leave you here then."

Defeated, Walker climbed onto the back of the creature. "Sometimes it's better not to know, Diesel."

"Clearly, that's your go-to policy," she said as she followed the 'vesters from a safe distance. "Maybe it's time to do things my way."

After a winding, slow ride through the ruins of the zone, the three players arrived at the Saint Mary Magdalene's Medical campus. And while the sprawling high-rises and parking garages spanned two city blocks, the facility had fallen into gross disrepair.

"The hospital of the damned," Walker said.

(Something about this place seems familiar.)

The 'vesters drove to the service entrance, through the loading dock, and out of sight.

"Okay, show's over," Walker said. "Let's go."

"No way." Diesel slid down the side of the beast and tied it to an overfilled bike rack. Standing in front of the automatic doors, a feeling of impending doom washed over her. Then she felt a wet and warm stickiness between her legs. She looked down and discovered a growing red spot on her crotch, lost among the many splatters of her enemies' blood.

(Impossible.)

"You're right, Walker. We should go."

By that time, her friends had already gone inside. Walker raided a supply closet and filled his backpack. Then he found a pair of surgical scrubs and tossed the clothes to Cheng. Diesel watched the automatic door close behind her friends as Cheng slipped out of his torn t-shirt and put on the blue short-sleeve, V-neck.

(He looks like a surgeon.)

The sticky spot between her legs felt odd.

(Numb.)

She got dizzy and broke out in a cold sweat. And then she remembered...

August 23, 2034.

Before Diesel knew what happened, the boot plunged a needle into her neck right above her yellow collar. He depressed the syringe.

Everything went black. Time marched on without her.

Groggy, when Diesel woke, an oxygen mask covered her face. A bluish figure stood over her calibrating something. Her dry eyes couldn't adjust to the bright operating room. Tight leather buckled around her wrists, binding her to the bed rails on each side. Suddenly alert, she kicked herself awake but felt resistance.

(THEY tied my ankles too.)

Starting at her belly button, a sharp pain shot through her gut and radiated into her back. Diesel would have doubled over, but being tied to the bed forced her to stay flat. It hurt more than anything she'd ever felt before, and she wanted to bolt.

"Shit. She's not supposed to be awake," a familiar female voice said.

The hovering blue blur fiddled with her settings. Holding a bloody scalpel, the familiar voice appeared and looked into Diesel's eyes. Still sedated and slipping under again, Diesel flinched at the creepy surgical disguise. Instead of the usual doctor's mask, this surgeon wore an oversized manic smile that stretched from ear to ear with long, skinny, sharp teeth.

(And no collar. I'm the only one wearing a collar.)

Right before she drifted under again, Diesel had one last thought.

(Her eyes look kind.)

The next time Diesel woke, the anesthesiologist had planned it. A new face floated over her hospital bed. This time it was the recovery nurse. She wore her black hair in braided cornrows.

(I like her hair. But no collar. She's got no collar either.)

The thick black woman wore an old-time uniform and one of those weird nurses' hats that look like a folded cloth napkin. Her white uniform strained at the buttons, making a gap over her bosom that exposed a tiny purple bow on her white bra.

"Where am I?"

"You're at Saint Mary Magdalene's Hospital, dear."

"Why? I'm not sick."

"Well, you bled, sweetheart. *They* can't have you bleeding, dear."

"I didn't try it. I'm sorry."

"I know, honey. But *They* took your uterus anyway. Your ovaries too."

"*They* took all my sex organs?"

(Of course THEY did. I couldn't really care.)

"Do I still have a vagina?"

The silly question made the black woman chuckle. Her deep belly laugh was infectious. Diesel couldn't help herself and giggled too, but the pain in her abdomen made her wince and stop.

"No. *They* didn't remove your vagina. You're still a girl, dear."

"Don't tell anyone. *They* don't like that I'm a girl."

"I know, sweetheart, I'm so sorry." The nurse held a cup of ice water for her and placed the bendy straw in Diesel's mouth. "You'll recover and feel great in no time. And just think, no more periods for you."

She sipped and swallowed, "Periods?"

"I guess it's kind of late and pointless to explain all that now, dear. All that matters is that you won't bleed again."

"No more blood for me?"

Smiling, the nurse nodded. "No more blood for you."

Now. Night.

(But now there is blood. Again.)

Diesel watched the red stain spread across her crotch.

(Showing my blood where no blood is supposed to be.)

Fortunately, her enemies' gore covered her from head to tink-tink.

"I'm showered in it."

(No one will notice one more spot. Even if it's THAT kind of blood. Even if it's THERE.)

"You look like Carrie after winning Prom Queen." Walker cringed.

(He didn't notice. It doesn't hurt. Only feels wet. And kinda numb down there.)

Soon she forgot about the resurrection of her menstrual period. Diesel navigated through the hospital maze of corridors and made it to the basement with her friends in no time. With their backs pressed against the wall, Diesel peeked at the automatic sliding doors around the corner. She read the word printed on the glass aloud, "Morgue."

Cheng asked, "Are you sure you want to see this, Diesel?"

"Is this where the 'vesters brought the bodies?"

"Yes," Walker answered.

Diesel spotted the surveillance. "Shouldn't we black out the camera or something? Are we out of Silly String?"

"It wouldn't make a difference. *They* know we're here. And *They* don't care," Walker said.

"It is not like we can do anything about it," Cheng said.

"It? About what?"

"Well, that's the ten-thousand dollar question, isn't it?" Walker said as he stopped trying to conceal himself and casually strolled through the sliding doors.

"Wait," Diesel whispered as she followed. "I'd much rather we go back to hiding. This doesn't feel right."

"I agree with Diesel." Hyper-vigilant, Cheng side-stepped along the wall.

Walker held his arms out at his side and spun in a full circle. "*They* don't care. We're just wasting time. Trust me."

"Well, I *do* care," Diesel snipped. "And I've had enough of your shit for one night. Now get your drunk ass back here against the wall."

"Fine." Walker complied. "Why don't you lead the way, then?"

The sound of a table saw echoed through the hall.

"What was that?" Diesel whispered.

"Just the harvesters harvesting," Walker slurred and smiled.

"The sound came from in there." Cheng pointed at a pair of double swinging doors with porthole windows in each.

The players crept toward the sound. Diesel pushed on a door, opening the rubber flap an inch, just wide enough for everyone to peer inside. Three covered bodies awaited on metal autopsy tables. Square stainless steel hatches covered an entire wall. Commercial kitchen counters with strange power tools lined the perimeter of the room. A bald attendant with no eyebrows wore a rubber butcher's apron, chainmail gloves, and galoshes, as she slushed through blood puddles on the tile floor. The woman lifted a blue sheet, revealing her next project.

"Wyatt," Diesel said to herself. Remembering the punches, she rubbed the back of her head.

(It was him or me. Like Bull said, "Every man for himself." Poor Wyatt, he didn't realize that EVERYMAN would be a WOMAN. Couldn't have happened to a better guy. I wonder where Bull is now.)

Then she noticed the odd clothing under the mortician's apron. The attendant wore an ankle-length black tunic that buttoned up high around her neck.

(And no compliance collar. Can't trust anyone without a collar.)

Underneath the goth cloak, the frilly white cuffs of the mortician's shirt purposely got in the way, soaking up blood from her chainmail gloves. The longer Diesel watched, the more erratic and hypnotic the morgue attendant moved. Sometimes, she worked in slow motion, and others she skipped like a film on fast forward. Unnaturally pale, her pasty white skin hadn't been exposed to sunlight in years. Burgundy and purple splotched her sunken eyes. Her eyes were red.

(Not bloodshot. Red irises. Disturbing.)

Diesel searched her memory for the right word from the book.

"Is she an *albino?*"

"No," Cheng answered as he retreated from the doorway and hid around the corner. "She is something entirely different, something much, much worse."

Using an odd key, the morgue-spook unlatched and removed Wyatt's dormant compliance collar. She snapped the lock and dropped the clear hoop over an old-fashioned barber's pole.

Sensing the collar, a red stripe swirled around the pole to signal acceptance. Wyatt's collar flashed white once, indicating that it had been deactivated as it fell onto an orderly stack of at least a dozen others.

"Is she recycling?" Diesel whispered.

Walker snickered at her choice of words, then nodded.

The gothic butcher chose a #22 scalpel and an aneurysm hook from her tray, then sliced into Wyatt's jugular. She fished an L-shaped tool into the neck incision, caught the artery, and raised it to the surface. After clamping and slicing open the thick vein, her nose twitched like a cat that caught a whiff of prey on a breeze. She trembled. Her mouth opened so wide that her jaw unhinged like a feeding boa constrictor. Diesel expected fangs, but the morgue creeper had no teeth at all.

(Her mouth is a dark hole. The blackest thing I've ever seen.)

From deep in the freak's throat, a proboscis appeared. It twisted through the air toward Wyatt's neck. The tip of a bizarre sucker wrapped around the severed artery and made a tight seal.

(What IS that thing?)

The creature drank and drained Wyatt dry. Then the organ released and retracted into the parasite's throat. The mortician creature ripped a loud burp, re-hinged her jaw, and closed her mouth. Calm and composed, she selected a meat cleaver from her tool tray and butchered Wyatt.

Diesel stepped away from the door, and her friends followed to huddle in the hallway.

"All right Cheng, it's time you tell me, what *IS* that—thing?"

"There are no words for it," Cheng said.

"No kidding." Unable to stop herself, Diesel peeked through the round window again. Then gestured for the guys to join her by the door. "Will you get over here?"

"No. I should not. She will sense me," Cheng objected.

"Sense you? Cheng, What is that creature?"

"There are no words for her kind in your language, or any Earth language for that matter." Cheng tapped his sunglasses a few times to scroll through his options. "The closest translation I can find is 'Space Vampire.'"

"Space vampire? You've got to be kidding," Diesel whispered.

"Just another night in Nevadaland," Walker mumbled.

The table saw interrupted their conversation. Curious, Diesel peeked. The space vampire disemboweled Wyatt and lifted him onto a workbench with ease. The mortician chopped him into chunks that resembled pot roasts. The butcher lined up a row of styrofoam trays, dealt out clean blood pads, and placed each cut of Wyatt with care. She wrapped the meat in plastic film and stepped on a pad that heated the table top and sealed the packages shut one-by-one. Finally, she slapped an orange "ration" sticker on top. Diesel spun back to her friends.

(Do NOT barf. Be quiet.)

"Rations are dead people?" Diesel gagged on the words.

"Yes. Meat became too expensive many years ago. The dead cost nothing," Cheng said.

"Especially if the bodies don't need to be buried," Walker added.

"You guys knew about this all along?"

The men nodded, as the saw buzzed.

"Why didn't you tell me?"

"Tell you that you've been fed human beings your whole life," Walker said. "Would you have believed me?"

"I guess not." Diesel took a deep breath. "What about you, Cheng? Do aliens eat people?"

"I suppose some species do," Cheng said. "But I do not eat vertebrates."

"You don't eat vertebrates?" Diesel asked. "Then what *do* you eat?"

"I was ready to eat the tentacle." A cockroach scuttled by and Cheng snatched it up, then swallowed it whole. "But these will have to do."

(That did not just happen.)

Diesel gagged again. The meat saw went silent. Cheng held a finger in front of his lips to warn her to be quiet. Inside the morgue, the blood sucking mortician moved on to the next body. She lifted another blue sheet to reveal the bisected Chickenman. Sniffing, her nose wrinkled in disgust. She replaced the cover. The offended space sucker considered her options and then slipped out a side door.

"Wait. So if everyone, and I mean everyone except some aliens, in Nevadaland is a cannibal—" Diesel paused to ponder her next words. "And you're trying so hard *NOT* to eat people, that means you're actually a good guy, Walker."

He smiled. "Well, thank you for finally saying so. I don't know about the rest of Nevadaland, or even about everyone in Reno. But I do know that all Reno rations are human meat. And thank you for forgiving me, Diesel."

"I didn't say I forgave you."

Walker frowned. "Well, I do try *SO* hard not to eat—"

"It might take me some time to get over the fact that you ate my leg—"

Cheng ran into the morgue and swiped a handful of halos from the barber pole.

"Cheng?" Diesel chased after him.

Walker did not follow. Cheng slid two dormant compliance collars under his cargo pants and started on the third when his head perked like a dog that heard a silent whistle.

"*They* are coming."

February 13, 2021.

Trey stared at the yellow stain from his two-week-old piss, then looked back at his frozen daughter's corpse. "Nina. I'm so sorry."

"Apologizing to the dead?" Ghost Jerome appeared to vex him again, "How come I never get one of these world famous expressions of regret from my own son? Huh, Professor?"

"Shut it, old man." Trey opened the door to the death car. For the first time since becoming snowbound, the inventory had decreased. A pile of stripped bones grew in the corner.

(I thought Gizmo and I could eat like kings forever. And now, looking at this... Well, maybe not forever. That was two weeks ago. Fourteen days ago, Gizmo and I started eating Amara. She's all gone now. My wife is gone. Consumed. And now the other survivors. They've discovered my secret. I thought if they knew I ate her, they'd turn on me. I never imagined they'd join me. That surviving would mean becoming accomplices.)

Trembling, he closed the door and returned to his child. Walker brushed a stray curl out of his dead girl's frozen face. His hands shook so bad from the cold that his loving gesture came off more like a drunken pawing. Nina sunk further into the packed snow between the rest of the train car and the—

"Dining car," Zombie Pops shuffled his feet in a little soft shoe as he vamped for an audience that was not there. "Where's my high hat after the punchline, Professor?"

Walker did not respond, but his teeth chattered.

"You let me down, son," the rotting corpse said. His sagging lip drooped as he frowned.

"W-why dd-dd-don't ya-you g-gg-go away?"

"You better warm up, or you'll wind up with frozen bones too," corpse daddy opened the door to the smoky residential car. Pungent body odor wafted into the in-between space.

"I cc-cc-can't leave her. Someone ww-ww-will eat her," Walker forced the words out between his chattering teeth.

"I'll watch Nina."

Walker gave his dead father a distrustful look.

"Go, Professor. Go." Zombie Pops stood in front of his dead grandchild with his arms spread wide.

Reluctant, Walker snuck into the dormer car, hoping no one would notice him. He passed a dirty woman bundled in layers of ratty and torn clothes.

(Is she sleeping? Or dead?)

For a moment, he stared at her red faux-fur coat.

(Is her chest rising and falling? I can't tell. Is she breathing? Or is it my imagination?)

Unconvinced either way, he moved forward.

(It doesn't matter. Alive? Dead? I really don't care anymore.)

Walker warmed himself by the metal briefcase fire. Curled and cozy, Gizmo slept nearby with a full belly. Walker removed his gloves and placed them by the fire to dry, then affectionately petted his cat. Gizmo opened one eye, recognized his master, and stretched out his paw to cover his face. Holding his trembling hands over the flame, Walker identified the fuel—not by sight, but he knew.

(Smells like burning hair.)

Lounging with Gizmo, Walker lost track of time in a moment that seemed as close to normalcy as he could remember. But something snapped him back from his warm fantasy, and he bolted for the train door. Startled by his master's sudden move, Gizmo jumped straight up into the air. When Walker returned to the in-between space, he discovered the woman in the dreaded red coat down on all fours in the snow, gnawing a chunk out of Nina's ankle.

"Bitch!" Walker spat as he kicked the woman in the ribs.

(Of course, Dad's nowhere to be found. Asshole.)

The cannibal woman cackled like a wicked witch on her knees. "The little ones are so tender, even when frozen. It's a texture thing." She licked her lips.

Walker kicked the woman in the chin, splattering blood in the snow beside Nina, "That's my daughter. Have some respect, woman!"

Bleeding, she crawled into the doorway of the dining car and gestured inside, "But you helped me eat *MY* daughter. Remember? You should. It was only three days ago."

The image of a white teen girl entered his mind. And breast meat.

(I hate myself.)

"I vow to you, here and now. If I survive this, I'll never eat another human being as long as I live."

Hysterical, the woman laughed at his hopeful lie.

Now. Later.

The hairless mortician returned to her butcher shop morgue. And this time, the space vampire wasn't alone, another woman dressed in bloody surgical scrubs and a crazy mask followed her.

(I know that manic smile. That mask. And something about that woman's eyes.)

The surgeon pulled off her gruesome disguise.

"Ernesta," Diesel gasped from her hiding spot behind the swinging doors.

"Do you know her?" Cheng asked.

"She was a friend." Shocked, Diesel processed the memory of her time in the hospital.

Walker peeked through the portal window. "You have an odd taste in friends."

"Tell me about it." Diesel rolled her eyes.

Inside the morgue, the two women pushed Chickenman's autopsy table toward a power station on the wall. The morbid medics propped his head and torso onto a wedge.

"Have you drained him?" Ernesta asked.

"With this, I could not," the space vampire's voice sounded modulated, mechanically altered and lowered with more bass than a woman should have been able to speak. "In him, I sensed danger. I could not feed."

"All right then, I just don't want this to get messy. But since this creature already bled out, it shouldn't be too bad." Ernesta slipped on latex gloves and pulled her manic-grin mask over her face. Then she put on a visor with an oversized splash guard that looked like half a transparent lampshade. She flipped several switches and pushed some buttons, and an array of LED indicators lit the power station. Plugging in a handheld rotary saw, she then turned on the power. It made a higher and faster sound than the table saw.

Without drawing guidelines, Ernesta cut around the circumference of the red comb on Chickenman's head. Exchanging her rotary saw for a stainless steel hook, she pried at the incision. His skullcap popped open. Grasping the rooster comb like a handle, she tossed the cranium bone. It landed in a bin full of garbage gore from other corpses.

Using a scalpel, Ernesta sliced through his brain sac and peeled away the membrane. She retrieved two electrodes that looked like acupuncture needles with curly wires coming out the end. Then she pushed the sharp electrodes deep into opposite sides of the gray matter. Ernesta nodded at the morgue vampire, who then flipped a switch on the power station.

Wide awake, Chickenman's eyes popped open. His eyelids fluttered.

"Are you recording?" Ernesta asked.

The space vampyress checked her monitors. "Affirmative."

Ernesta double checked. "Excellent."

The night butcher sniffed the air like a ravenous predator. She licked her lips as she followed the scent trail. "In you, I feel so hungry."

"Shit. The vampire's coming." Diesel scurried away from the door and dashed for the exit.

"It is too late. Once she detects me, she will not stop," Cheng said.

"What? She smells you?" Walker asked.

"My species is irresistible to her kind," Cheng said. He stepped into the center of the hallway, placed both hands on his hips, and awaited the inevitable conflict. "It desires my morphing flexibility. It hates being trapped as a human."

"What's wrong with being a human?" Walker asked.

"Humans are the most immutable species on Earth." Cheng glared down the hall.

Diesel tugged at him miming a jogging motion, "We can run. We should run."

"I am afraid not this time, Diesel."

The space vampire swung both doors open in a dramatic fashion and stepped through, "In you, I feel so hungry." Its modulated voice sounded evil and deliberate.

Walker backed down the hallway alone. "Shit, Cheng. She's coming for you."

"Yes, I know."

Cheng held his position. The bald woman's mouth opened wide as she unhinged her jaw. Her proboscis slithered out of her throat like a slimy elephant trunk. Diesel gagged. It seemed excited by Cheng.

"Run, Cheng!" Diesel yelled as the proboscis reared up and struck.

With extraordinary reflexes, Cheng choked the eight-foot long proboscis, keeping it inches from his face. Static electricity filled the air, lifting the little hairs on Diesel's arms. Tiny snaps flared and flashed through the hallway. Then lightning bolts flew out of Cheng's hands and into the monster's sucker. The parasite's snout seized and flailed, but Cheng held his choking grip. Electricity flowed from Cheng, down the proboscis, and into the space vampire. She shook violently—electrocuted, and then collapsed. Tendrils of blue smoke floated upward from the mortician's corpse.

"You killed it." Diesel stepped in for a closer look.

Walker remained quiet and kept his distance. Cheng drew his tactical knife and stood wide over his victim's head. The slender organ quivered as the host's corpse heaved.

(Dead things don't vomit.)

The proboscis ejected from the morgue creeper's throat followed by a bloated blood-sack shaped like a human stomach.

(But three times the size.)

The dead parasite landed on the hospital floor with a splat.

Diesel prodded it with the tip of her tink-tink. "It's dead right?"

"The vampire is dead, but soon we will have another problem."

(Ernesta?)

Diesel stepped toward the morgue. "I have to talk to her," she whispered.

The corpse reached out and grabbed Diesel's ankle. It squeezed with such force that the chainmail gloves dug deep into her flesh. Diesel screamed in both shock and pain. Without hesitation, Cheng plunged his knife deep into the host's skull. The blow to the brain killed it.

(Again.)

"Like a zombie." Walker crept out from the shadows.

Diesel kicked free from the death grip of the corpse. While the guys studied the dead creature, she limped into the morgue.

"Ernesta?" Diesel announced her presence with a child-like lack of confidence.

The surgeon spoke through her creepy mask without looking up from her work, "Yes, Diesel?"

"You remember me? Recognize me?"

"Of course I do."

A picture of a long ago memory flashed into Diesel's mind.

(My first Christmas.)

She envisioned Ernesta sitting on the bed with her, enjoying all the colors of her new Deluxe Art Set. Then it dawned on her.

(She wore no collar. She was a housekeeper. A servant. She should have had a yellow collar.)

Diesel searched her other memories, focusing on Ernesta's neck.

(She never wore a collar.)

"How could I miss that?" Diesel said aloud.

"*THEY* know you're here, Diesel." Ernesta poked an electrode around Chickenman's brain.

"You told them?"

(Such betrayal.)

"No."

"I thought you were my friend."

"I was your handler."

"Handler?"

"You were an assignment, Diesel." Ernesta turned to the power station and recorded data from the creature's brain.

"Then why would you bring me presents?" Diesel fought back tears.

"*THEY* wanted you to have the paints."

"But *WHY?* I don't understand."

"Do you have an opinion? 'Yes,' or 'No,'" Ernesta asked.

"What's that supposed to mean?"

"Yes or no?" Ernesta repeated.

Brandishing his knife, Cheng dashed past Diesel and sliced deep into Ernesta's throat. He hacked and sawed until her head popped off. The surgeon's body collapsed behind the autopsy table.

"Cheng, *NO!*" Diesel screamed. Then she paused.

(No blood. Wait. Why not?)

Not ready to see the gore, Diesel crept forward anyway.

(I loved her.)

Walker entered the morgue again. Reluctant, Diesel peeked around the table, avoiding the sight of Chickenman's open skull. Ernesta lumped into a pile of her own severed wires and broken circuits.

"She was not human, Diesel." Cheng took evidence pictures of Chickenman with his augmented reality glasses.

Diesel cried.

Walker looked at the humanoid pile on the ground. He touched Diesel on the elbow, "She was *THEY.*" Then he grabbed Ernesta's head and plopped it onto the autopsy table between the chicken feet. He tore off her splatter shield and mask.

"I don't get it. *WHY?*"

Cheng fiddled with the power station and pushed some buttons until he found the data recordings. "*THEY* are learning. That is what artificial intelligence does. It learns."

"Yes. It's what *They* do," Walker agreed.

Cheng placed both hands on the power station, concentrated, and fried the circuits with his remaining electricity.

"About that," Diesel said. "How come you never did *that* before?"

"Discharge is extremely draining." Cheng pulled a small bottle of antifreeze-colored liquid from the pocket of his cargo pants. He chugged. "Discharge is for emergencies only. I think I had enough left to knock out the communication link."

"Enough zappy zap?" Walker asked.

"I think so." Cheng nodded as he tossed the empty bottle across the room and into the gore bin. "That was my last dose of extract."

"*They* know everything." Walker pulled Ernesta's long braid out of its twisted bun. He slung the humanoid's decapitated noggin over his shoulder and held the braid like a rope.

Still stunned, Diesel stared at him in disbelief. "What?"

The friends' collars all buzzed at the same time.

An automated announcement blasted over the hospital PA system. "The first player has entered the Coliseum. Congratulations to Nikolai Bull." Studio recorded applause followed the warning announcement.

(He did it.)

"We are running out of time," Cheng said.

Diesel bolted. The guys followed. When the players made it back to the hospital entrance, the Medusapotamus was gone. But the bike rack remained.

"The beast must have broken loose and wandered away," Cheng said.

Walker yanked on a bicycle locked to the rack. "How about some help?"

Diesel changed attachments and popped on her saw-leg. She flexed and revved and cut through the U-lock. Walker wrestled the beat up mountain bike free from the tangle of others.

Diesel cut more.

Cheng threaded the severed cable through the handle of a self-breaking, ultra-balanced hoverboard. Unlike the antique ones that caught fire and didn't actually hover, this one floated four inches above the pavement when he switched on the power.

An old-fashioned kick scooter drew Diesel's eye. Still limping, she stepped on board with her bloody foot and used her saw-leg like a motorized wheel. She sped half-way down the block before the guys even moved.

She yelled back at her friends, "Come on, we have to hurry."

The Keepers

June 4, 2037. Sunrise.

Leading the way, Diesel hung a left on 4th Street.

Walker paused and pointed north toward Evans Street. "Hey, Diesel, the Coliseum's this way."

She yelled without even turning around, "I have to make a pitstop first."

Without pausing, Cheng glided past Walker on his humming hoverboard and followed her.

"But—" Walker turned north, then he looked at Diesel again. He readjusted Ernesta's head, hiking it further up his shoulder. "You'll be the death of me, girl."

The guys played follow-the-leader for a few blocks, while Diesel revved her saw-leg so fast that she kicked up sparks, leaving a carved trail in the road. By the time she reached the Big Top

Hotel and Casino, she had ground her blade toothless. Getting to be a pro at swapping attachments, she jumped off her scooter and switched to her tink-tink before Walker and Cheng caught up to her. The guys ditched the bike and hover board by the front doors, while she stashed her saw-leg in its holster.

"Why did you bring us here?" Cheng asked.

"I have to see my mural."

"What?" Walker asked.

"My mural," Diesel repeated. "I always see it in my head when I close my eyes, but I have to see it now. I need to see what *They* did to it."

The players rushed into the smoky casino lobby.

"This is where we all met." Walker acted odd, sentimental.

Diesel dashed through banks of slot machines, up the winding stairs, and onto the Midway with the guys following close behind. Free from their rooms, clusters of yellow-collared wards roamed the arcade with no money to spend. A few regs' poked around a Skill Crane trying to win the latest techno-gadget for a fraction of the cost. Carnies wore black collars and manned the fair games that nobody wanted to play.

(Bright colors. Forced festivity. "Fun, fun, FUN," screaming everywhere. And yet, nothing but desperate sadness.)

Diesel weaved through the maze of colorful ring-toss and water-gun booths until she found a security exit with no handles on the doors.

"We're going in there."

"Isn't that black-collar access only?" Walker asked.

"Call it a glitch." Diesel winked.

"A glitch?" Walker pondered it, fascinated. "Really?"

Diesel squeezed between the painted canvas of the baseball-pitch booth and the wall to a storage room. Cheng followed her.

"Now we wait," Diesel whispered.

"Hold on a sec." Walker detoured down an alley of carnival games.

"We do not have a lot of time for waiting," Cheng shout-whispered. "Players are making their way to the Coliseum right now."

Walker nodded as he dashed away. Making a beeline for the basketball booth, he slipped Ernesta's head over his shoulder and palmed her face. While running, he wrapped her long braid around her skull and tucked it. When the Midway worker spotted him, she danced a funky pop and lock. She whipped her long blonde hair in a clockwise circle around her black collar. Walker nodded, stepped up to the line, and lobbed a three-point jump shot.

"Nothing but net." Walker pumped his fist.

A scoop jutted out from behind the booth and collected Ernesta's severed robot head after it fell through the hoop. The package tumbled down the retracting shoot into a rolling laundry bin in one of the service tunnels. Another undercover ULCER operative received the deposit, covered it with dirty towels, and rolled it away to the Underground. Back on the Midway, Walker spun on his heels and sprinted back to his friends. He remembered the drills he ran with coach after school every day his junior year. Barely winded, he hid behind the baseball-pitch tent with Diesel and Cheng.

"Nice." Diesel offered him a high-five.

A baseball smacked the other side of the tent next to Walker's head before he could return the gesture. Startled, he asked, "*Now someone decides to play?*"

The door to the backstage tunnel opened, and a morbidly obese security guard strolled onto the Midway. Diesel dove out from behind the game booth and stuck her tink-tink in the door just before it slammed shut.

"Look who got her foot in the door."

"Shut up, Walker."

"I noticed you are no longer limping, Diesel." Cheng said.

Diesel looked down at her bloody ankle. "Huh? Oh. It doesn't hurt anymore. I forgot all about it. Guess it wasn't that bad." She popped the door open and held it for the guys.

The friends disappeared into the security access tunnel. Walker touched his collar, expecting it to buzz, but it didn't.

"I told you—glitch." Diesel led the guys deeper into the dark passage.

Bare fluorescent light fixtures and exposed electrical conduit ran across the blown-asbestos ceiling. Dead cockroach carcasses and cigarette butts littered cobwebs where the block walls met the cracked concrete floor.

"Don't you trust me?"

"I trust you. But I'm not sure this is a glitch," Walker said.

"Back at the river you risked your life for a *possible* glitch," Diesel said.

"It's just that *They* don't make mistakes."

"Glitch? Mistake? What's the difference? *They* insist I'm a male," Diesel said. "That's a mistake."

"Yes, but *THEY* did not make that mistake. Walker did."

"Will you shut up?" Walker shook his head. "She just stopped being pissed at me. Thanks a lot, man."

"Out with it, Walker," Diesel insisted, refusing to take them further.

"I may have been the data entry person that screwed up your gender in the system."

"'May have been?' Shit, Walker, do you just go around trying to find ways to quash me?"

"Quash?" Cheng repeated.

"No. I'm not trying to screw with you. Just shit happens, you know?"

"Right. I know. Shit just happens. Seems like it happens to some of us more than others, but whatever." Diesel led the guys through the tunnels and across intersections that led to kitchens and service elevators. Then she hung a right toward the stairwell. "This way. There's cameras in the elevators."

"Okay," Walker said.

Climbing over a dozen flights, the guys lost track, but Diesel didn't.

(Seventeen, and... Eighteen. Home sweet home.)

"Here we are." Diesel rushed through the exit door into the hallway that she had paced so many times in her childhood. Dim wall sconces lined the long corridor. Stained swirls of ornate flowers and repeating vines twisted into a surreal pattern on the floor. Another exit awaited at the other end of the hall far, far away. Diesel ran.

(Tink-tink feels different on carpet.)

She stopped when she got to her door. Nervous, she twisted the grippy rubber tip of her prosthetic into the nappy pile. Then she tapped what should have been her toe a few times.

(Feels so strange, being here.)

Cheng caught up to her with Walker close behind.

"This is it, guys. This is where I grew up."

"Are you going to go inside?" Cheng asked.

"What if someone else lives here now?" Diesel reached for the door handle, and her hand trembled. She paused. "It's probably locked."

(It was ALWAYS locked.)

"We've got your back, Dee."

"Dee?" Diesel smiled at Walker.

"I'm sorry, did that piss you off?"

"No. I kind of like it. You can call me that." Diesel pulled the lever handle.

Much to everyone's surprise, the door opened. The three friends stood shoulder-to-shoulder in the vestibule. Diesel pushed forward and looked inside.

"Whoa." Walker recognized a grid of blue laser lines over her entire mural. Projected blue flickers strobed in the dark hallway. "*They* are cataloguing."

Diesel stepped into her old room.

(Home.)

"So. *They* did send Ernesta. Because *They* wanted this," Diesel said.

Cheng followed, capturing images of the mural with his augmented reality glasses. "You drew Theta Rhonda Four."

"I did?" Diesel asked, "It's just home. I've never been there. But I just knew. I could see it." Diesel closed her eyes. "I still can."

"This is my home too." Cheng walked the perimeter, photographing Diesel's artwork.

"*They* took the furniture and curtains," Diesel said. "The room seems so big."

Mini-towers scattered through the room projected the laser grid onto the wall, ceiling, and floor. Mobile active scanners logged every inch of her painting.

Walker tapped his foot. "You even painted the floor."

"I sure did. I tore out that crummy carpet and painted the bare concrete."

"Every single surface is covered. You have painted every inch of baseboard, and every fixture, even the door knobs." Cheng paused, then photographed the pastel drawing on the window with his sunglasses, "This lava dome is called Mount Tarawera."

Walker's mouth hung open as he gazed at the ceiling, "Diesel, this is—"

"Amazing?" Diesel admired her work.

"I was going to say 'sad.' You were a prisoner."

"This didn't feel like a prison. This felt like home."

"You are right, Diesel. *They* want this." Walker fussed with one of the scanners.

"But why?"

"For the same reason *They* want Chickenman's brain," Walker said. "*They* are learning. Learning about the visitors."

"Visitors? I'm not a visitor. I was born here."

"That is true, but your father was one of us."

"How do you know about my father, Cheng?"

He pointed at his sunglasses, "I compiled an image search of the sketch you showed me back at the barracks. I found a link to his distress call."

A synthetic humanoid emerged from the bathroom. Its titanium skeleton and white fibrous robot muscles flexed with each step. Red almond-shaped eyes glowed behind a humanesque mask. Earhole sensors burrowed into the sides of its metallic skull. Its plastic nose and mouth were fused shut.

Walker recognized the model immediately. "A service droid. *They* don't bother adding skin to make these look human. We're in trouble."

It reached for Diesel. Without moving its mouth, the robot spoke with Inez's voice, "Come to Daddy."

No one in the room had ever met Inez, so no one recognized his voice. Still, the freaky choice affected Diesel. A chill ran down her spine.

(Creepy.)

The android waved its arm and all three of their collars turned red and vibrated.

"Shit," Diesel said.

Cheng kept taking photos with his glasses. Walker tackled the robot. As he struggled to wrestle and punch the humanoid, Diesel danced around like the floor was lava.

She yanked on her collar, "It's getting hot, Walker. *HOT!*"

"I know," Walker yelled as he clawed at the synth's rubbery abdomen. The robot choked him, and his hot collar melted into the hands of the android. Walker poked his fingers into the robot, penetrating deep. He tore at the fake muscle until he exposed a red button. Gasping for air, Walker punched the kill switch. The humanoid collapsed into sleep-mode, and all their collars switched back to blue.

"Why don't you change these to green so we can get the hell out of here? You know, so we can walk right out of the zone."

"If I could, I would, Dee." Walker pushed the dead machine away as he rolled over and crawled to his feet. "We have to get out of here. *They* will send more." He headed for the door. "Did you get what you needed? Because it's time to go."

"I guess. No, not really. I wanted answers. I'm not sure we got any. All I have is more questions."

"That's Nevadaland for you. Cheng, you about done, buddy?"

Cheng nodded, then snapped three more pictures of the ceiling before running after his friends. The players dashed out of the room. More synths appeared from the stairwell. Diesel heard a line of keepers drumming from behind.

Diesel turned. The drum line approached from the other end of the hall. Thick fur covered each drummer from the neck down. The keepers wore demon masks with protruding longhorns that overlapped and scraped against each other. Flattened gas tanks hung waist-high as each musician hammered with broken ax-handles wrapped in duct tape. The keepers stood shoulder-to-shoulder three wide and three deep. Thick with padding, their stump-like silhouettes swayed with the drumming.

"*They* are trying to keep us in the game," Diesel gasped.

"That's why *They* call 'em the keepers."

"*They* are like shepherds, and we are the sheep." Cheng turned and retreated.

"Quick, back inside." Walker ushered Diesel into the hotel room. He slammed and locked the door behind him.

"Now what?" Diesel asked.

Cheng grabbed one of the laser stands and heaved it at the window. It bounced back without breaking the glass. He slammed the metal legs into the window three more times before it finally broke. Mount Tarawera shattered, then fell into shards.

"We're eighteen floors up." Diesel stuck her head out. "I used to take the screws out to open this window as a kid. There's no way down from here."

"There were screws?" Cheng shrugged. Then he pushed a button on his glasses, "Yuki, are you there? Yuki, I am stuck. Yuki, I need you."

"We're trapped," Diesel said.

Walker crammed his face against the peephole. "I don't see them yet."

"Yuki, are you there?"

"Scratch that—the keepers are here," Walker announced.

Each of their collars flashed, and three players' names were announced through the PA system. The friends paused to listen.

"Do you know any of those guys?" Diesel asked.

"No," Walker said.

The keepers pounded on the door with wrapped ax handles.

"We're out of time." Walker lunged for the window. "Jump?"

"Eighteen floors? You're crazy," Diesel said. "We'll die."

"I can live with that," Walker said.

"Very funny." Diesel punched his arm.

The keepers banged and banged on the door. The room shook.

"Yuki, I NEED you," Cheng yelled into his sunglasses as he climbed onto the window frame, kicking out a shard of glass.

Diesel held her breath and watched it tumble.

(It's taking forever to hit.)

The glass crashed onto the pavement below and shattered, making the faintest sound.

Tink.

"No way. This is a bad idea." Diesel backed away.

A drone appeared outside to record all the action. The keepers broke through the door and filed into the room one-by-one.

"*They*'re here," Diesel said.

Cheng jumped.

"*CHENG, NO!*" Diesel screamed as she dove through the window after him.

She fell two stories when the griffin beast swooped in underneath. The two players tumbled on to the lion's back. Cheng landed in a riding position. But unprepared, Diesel fell face down across the rump of the beast. The creature flapped its enormous dragon wings.

Woosh, woosh. Woosh.

Air currents whizzed through her hair like tiny cyclones. Diesel pushed herself up to sit as the mutant-lion dragon circled around the hotel tower. Like the medusapotamus, she couldn't grip the beast with her tink-tink. The height made her woozy.

(I can't ride sideways. What if I FALL?)

She mimicked Cheng and spread her legs to mount like a normal rider.

(I need something to hold on to. Cheng? He's too far away. No chance. I'm not moving one inch.)

Out of reach, Cheng held on to the mutant's long mane. Diesel hunkered down and hugged the beast's back. The rhythmic motion of the Pterodactyl wings relaxed her.

(Hypnotic.)

Each time the wings flapped, Diesel bounced up and down.

(I'm so unstable. I don't like this feeling one bit. Especially, while—flying. OH my goddess. We're FLYING!)

Viewing the painted red-and-white-striped faux circus tent from high above, she imagined falling. The combination of this totally new perspective and the intense feeling of vulnerability gave birth to her new fear of heights.

(Acrophobia.)

On the approach toward the broken window, Cheng yelled at Walker, "You will have to jump."

Walker looked back at the keepers filling the room and eagerly agreed, "Okay." Balancing, he climbed into the window. He rocked back and forth anticipating the perfect timing. Then he leaped and landed on the back of the lion behind Diesel. The griffin beast's sixteen-foot-long reptilian tail wagged.

Walker flinched as the tip brushed by his face. "Snake? Why'd it have to be a snake?"

"Do not worry, it is not a snake," Cheng laughed.

"That's a lizard tail. Different reptile."

"Lucky me." Walker looked around nervously. Then he relaxed, "This griffinosaur sure beats a bicycle. Lots more room than the medusapotamus too. It's like flying first class."

"Griffinosaur?" Diesel asked.

"I just now named this beast. You know, part griffin, part dinosaur."

"Why not dragoniffin? You know, part dragon, part griffin?"

"Because I chose griffinosaur."

"Randomly. Just like that?"

"Yup. That's how it works."

"Who do you think you are? God or something?"

"Or something." Walker scratched his head.

The flying mutant landed on the roof of the Big Top Hotel and Casino parking garage. Yuki, an alluring drag queen in a gothic gown with an impressive black updo, glided toward the lion's mouth and stroked its nose. The beast purred as it nuzzled her.

(I remember her from the Bonanza. She wears an orange collar, but she's anything but regular.)

"Thank you, my darling Yuki."

She smiled. Without a word, Yuki strolled over to Cheng in her gigantic platform-heeled boots. She leaned in, and Cheng bent down and gave her a passionate kiss.

(I'm not jealous. Nope. Not me. But damn, she's gorgeous. More beautiful than any of the pink-collared hopefuls at the Bonanza. She puts all the girls to shame.)

"We're running out of time. We need to get to the Coliseum." Walker interrupted the couple's reunion.

Cheng and Yuki parted. She stared through his dark glasses, holding his gaze. He couldn't, and didn't want to, take his eyes off her.

"Can you help us?"

Nodding, Yuki stroked Cheng on the cheek, then leaned forward and whispered something in the lion's ear. In a second, the griffinosaur took off and flew directly toward their destination, leaving Yuki behind.

"Whoa, that's some Beast Master shit," Walker said.

"She is more like a beast mistress," Cheng corrected.

Yuki smiled from the ground as she waved goodbye.

The Coliseum

June 4, 2037.

"There it is, Diesel, the Coliseum," Walker shouted, pointing over her shoulder as the friends glided on the back of the griffinosaur. "Are you ready for this?"

"Of course I am," Diesel said. "It's what comes next."

"You're probably gonna have to kill someone to get in."

Diesel responded without pause, "If forced to choose between them or me, I will always choose me."

Recalling his winter buried inside the train, Walker nodded. "Yes, that's what survivors do."

From a block away, she heard the groans of the dying. The Coliseum looked like any ordinary mid-tier college stadium, except it had the familiar Nevadaland patina of urban decay.

"It used to have a roof, but *They* tore it off so the drones could fly in and out to cover the gladiator fights," Walker said.

(That gives me an idea.)

Diesel lunged forward to tell Cheng. Her tink-tink slipped, exposing a deformed growth bud where her kneecap used to be. The scaly, pink and green tumor throbbed.

(No wonder my harness hasn't been fitting right.)

"We should fly right in. Why fight if we don't have to?" She rested her chin on his shoulder.

Cheng smiled, "I like the way you think, Diesel, but this beast will land where Yuki instructed. I do not control it."

The ground wiggled and bled below as the players began their descent toward the main entrance of the Coliseum. A swarm of drones hovered near the ground, capturing all the gruesome battle action. Stretching for a better view, Diesel bumped her loose prosthetic against the pterodactyl wing. One of her straps broke, and her metal leg flopped everywhere. Without thinking she grabbed for tink-tink, lost her balance, and fell off the griffinosaur. Walker lunged forward, grasping for Diesel, but he was too late. She slipped away.

(I'm falling.)

"Cheng, she fell! Go *BACK* and get her!"

Cheng turned, shocked to see Diesel gone. "I cannot control this beast." Cheng pulled on the lion's mane, trying to steer the mutant like he did the medusapotamus. But he only angered the griffinosaur. It hissed fire and growled.

A fresh corpse broke Diesel's fall. On impact, the last leather strap holding her tink-tink snapped. Her prosthetic fell between a dying player writing in pain and a detached torso. Diesel scrambled to reach around an oozing shoulder stump for her attachment. Right before dying, a wounded guy bit her, but he didn't break the skin. Then his collar went dormant as two-hundred pounds of his dead weight buried her lost leg. Standing on the back of another corpse, the bloody bride appeared in front of her.

"I will guide you, Diesel. Follow me."

"But I can't walk."

"There's no walking through this. You'll have to crawl your way out."

Diesel craned her neck to look past Amelia. Only death and pain lay ahead, at least a hundred yards of it, all the way to the Coliseum. Cattle-chute pedestrian fences forced everyone through the same narrow corridor. Orange collars mixed with blue, most fading into colorlessness, as both regs' and players died in agony.

"Why would regs' come here? Now?" Diesel whispered to herself.

(To cheat. To influence the games. To win the bets.)

Amelia interrupted her thought, "Don't worry about it, Diesel."

(THEY always set us up like this. Set us up for more drama. Force us to fight and set us up to lose. It looks like a goddamn battlefield.)

Amelia screeched like a howling banshee, "It *IS* a battlefield. Now move!"

Diesel pushed with her good leg and pulled with her arms.

(I feel like a three-legged spider. Probably look like one too.)

"Get out of your head! Pay attention, damn it. Stop worrying about what you look like, and hustle, woman! You are all *ALONE* out here. No family. No friends. Only enemies. Someone could come up behind you and kill you at any moment. Time to amp up the energy. No more playing around. This is *WAR! Now MOVE soldier.*" Amelia's face turned from pretty and pale to aged and dark, making the ghost-woman look like a rotting corpse.

Diesel couldn't get a good grip or solid footing. Every time she moved, dead bodies shifted under her. She dripped sweat. Wet spots spread into bloodstains on her clothes. Huffing and puffing, she worked harder than ever before.

(Work smarter, not harder.)

Despite her busted thigh harness, Diesel reached for the mantis attachment in her back pack. She removed her thigh belt and then made a fist around the mantis socket. She wrapped the strap tight around her hand, then pulled the buckle tight with her teeth.

Dead Amelia smiled. "That's my girl."

Diesel punched forward and her mantis leg extended all the way, piercing a torso two bodies ahead of her. She flexed her hand and the insect limb contracted, pulling her into the air and propelling her forward. Repeating this pneumatic process, Diesel skipped over the dead like a manic pole-vaulter. A desperate player grabbed at her ankle, but couldn't hold his grip as she launched herself into the air again.

(I've got this. I can DO this.)

The griffinosaur landed on the steps near the ticket booth where gladiator Kali guarded the finish line at the VIP entrance. Players attacked Cheng and Walker before the men had a chance to dismount the beast. Cheng fought through, slicing and dicing with his tactical blade and managing to poach weapons from two opponents. He kept nunchucks for himself and tossed a spiked chain at Walker. The lion-head chewed the arm off a reg' dumb enough to stumble across the griffinosaur's path. The gruesome diversion distracted the goaltending Kali, and a lucky player slipped past the finish line.

The collars on all the living flashed once, and the PA system made an announcement, "Blair Downey."

(Five spots left. Then we ALL lose.)

Frustrated by defeat, goddess Kali howled.

Mesmerized by her favorite white-collar, Diesel landed elbow deep in the guts of an eviscerated player at the bottom of the steps.

(Ugh. So slippy. And the smell!)

Diesel gagged. She closed her eyes to keep from puking. Cheng bashed a reg' in the head with his nunchuck. The orange-collar wobbled.

"You are almost here, Diesel. Keep going," Cheng shouted.

(I can't fight Kali. She's a gladiator. She's a goddamn goddess. I'm just. A broken mess. I don't know if I can do this.)

"Move it, sister!" Amelia screamed in her ear. "Now is NOT the time for doubt. Now. *UP!*" One step at a time, Amelia showed Diesel the path of least resistance.

"Keep going, Diesel," Cheng shouted as he punched his opponent.

Diesel followed the ghost bride's guidance. After crawling up the steps, she hoisted herself up by the hand rail and stood on her one leg. Behind her, players battled on a field of the dead. In front of her, Cheng fought a blood-soaked reg', while Walker wrestled with another player. Then the griffinosaur's ears perked up. The beast flew away, and Diesel focused on the nine-foot-tall Kali.

The blue-green goddess stood three feet in front of the red laser finish line. She had one job, to kill anyone who tried to pass. Kali's skirt of shriveled human arms had decayed more since the last time Diesel ogled her at the Bonanza. The angry goddess picked off players one-by-one as each tried to cross the goal line. An interfering reg' got too close, and Kali choked him with her two upper hands. With her lower arms, she lifted him high. The puny human tugged on her helmet, so she tore off his arm. Then for fun, she ripped off the rest of his limbs. The goddess of rage finished by flipping the body, popping off its head, and flinging the torso down the stairs. Next, the gladiator chose the guy pinning Walker down.

Behind Kali. Behind the finish line. Inside the Coliseum. Diesel made eye contact with an old friend.

(Bull.)

"Hurry, Diesel. Now, while Kali's distracted," Safe, Bull coached from inside the arena.

Just a few feet from Kali, Diesel nodded and hopped toward him.

(What's that smell? Onions? And lavender. Is that what a goddess smells like? Yuck.)

When Diesel made her move, her collar flashed white and vibrated. She tugged at it and said, "I'm being paged."

Bull shrugged. "I can't come back out there." He pointed at his blue collar. "Once we cross the line, we can't go back."

"*Why* am I being paged? Who's doing this?" Diesel turned toward the battlefield. Angel blasted through the barricade, galloping on the medusapotamus.

(That's Cheng's harness. Angel stole the beast. That bastard.)

Without discriminating, the creature trampled the living and dead alike.

"Damn it, quit changing the rules," Diesel screamed at a drone that zoomed in for a close-up of her reaction.

Quartering the other player, Kali hissed behind her, and Diesel hopped away. Walker stepped in between to fight the goddess.

"How am I supposed to win, if you keep changing the rules?" Diesel yelled in frustration.

The bloody bride glided by with her ever-evil grin.

Kali laughed, a deep, evil laugh, much more masculine than any woman should sound, "Who said you're supposed to win?"

Halfway through the corridor, players attacked Angel from all sides. He flung off the blinders and yanked the reins left. The medusapotamus plodded in a circle. Its stump-like foot squashed the skull of a dead man like a ripe melon. As the mutant trampled, its eyes turned three players to stone.

"Do *NOT* look at it, Diesel," Cheng yelled. "Diesel, look at *ME!*" Cheng stabbed another attacker at the gate.

"But I'm being paged."

Amelia danced like a macabre ballerina and fluttered her fingers to keep Diesel's attention away from the beast.

Angel charged the steps and rammed Kali. Seizing the opportunity, two more players slipped through the gate. The stunned gladiator floundered and flailed her eight limbs, looking like a spider flipped on its back. Recovering by hugging the mutant's neck, the goddess crammed her claws into its face. She pierced its mystical eyeballs and plucked them out of the beast's skull. In pain, the medusapotamus reared up on its hind legs, tossing Angel to the ground. Whining, the beast trotted away crushing bodies with each step. All blue collars flashed twice. The PA system announced two names Diesel didn't know.

(Only three spots left.)

Everyone switched back to blue, but Diesel's collar kept flashing white and vibrating. "Cheng?"

"Do not panic. It is not red."

"Diesel!" Angel screamed as he approached. "You killed Randall. And now it's time for you to die." His collar flashed white too.

Ignoring Walker, Kali moved to attack Diesel. "Time for you," the goddess howled with a piercing screech.

Walker jumped between Kali and Diesel again. He stood several feet shorter than the gladiator with his only weapon—the spiked chain. The skulls of her necklace rolled across her heaving naked breasts as she cackled at his pathetic display.

(He can't win.)

Walker whipped Kali, but she swatted the chain away like an annoying housefly. The goddess punched him four times with an otherworldly combo. Cheng attacked Kali from behind. She hit him square in the chest with a spinning backfist that knocked him off his feet. Cheng flew backward, and when he landed, he had crossed the threshold into the Coliseum. All the players' collars flashed white once, and the PA system announced his name, "Gan Cheng."

"No!" Cheng dashed back toward the fight.

Bull grabbed him by the arm and held him back. "You can't go. Your collar will blow."

Diesel shouted at her battling friend, "Only two more spots, Walker. We need to move!"

Walker dove to the ground and stabbed Kali in her bare foot with the spike. The goddess of wrath howled with rage. Walker wiggled and crammed the metal point through her foot. She bled black as he threaded the chain through her. Circling her, Walker pulled the chain tight. With her pierced foot twisted around her calf, Kali fell face-first onto the concrete. Walker jumped onto her back, yanked off her gold helmet, and bashed her head into the ground. After knocking her unconscious, Walker crammed his knees into Kali's spine to keep her down. He grabbed a fistful of her luxurious black hair and twisted it around his hand twice.

(Control the head and control the body.)

Angel moved in on Diesel. In defense, she raised her mantis as a shield. Angel scoffed as he drew his 9 mm semi-automatic from inside his waistband. He pointed the laser mounted sight on her forehead and smiled at the red dot.

"How'd you get a gun?"

"How do I get any of the things I get?" Angel answered. "Randall got it for me."

"Who's Randall?"

"Chickenman, bitch," Angel answered in disgust. "He had a name, you know. And his name was Randall."

"That's how it goes in the games, Angel." Walker knelt on Kali's back. "Every man for himself. You know that."

"That's right." Angel kept his sights set on Diesel. Without dropping the muzzle of his pistol, he sidestepped all the dead bodies and crept past Kali. Diesel froze.

(He's going to kill us. First, me. Then Walker. He hates everyone.)

Angel's finger moved from the pistol's frame to the trigger. Diesel held her breath waiting for his next move.

(Can I take him out with the mantis? Knock the gun out of his hand? I doubt it. He'll shoot me if I twitch.)

"No." Angel held the gun on Diesel, as he backed toward the finish line. "Shooting you now, that's too easy. Everything is so easy for you."

"Easy?" Diesel blurted. "Damn, are you kidding?" Diesel hopped on one foot. "Does this look easy to you?"

"I want to watch you die the same way you killed Randall." Angel stepped toward the gate. "Painfully. Yes. With lots of blood. At my hand." Angel stepped across the red laser line and entered the Coliseum. Satisfied, he holstered his gun. When he turned, Cheng greeted him with a punch to the face. Angel just laughed, then tapped Cheng's sunglasses, leaving a greasy fingerprint on the center of the lens before walking into the shadows.

The blue-collars flashed once, and the PA system announced his name, "Angel Rodriguez."

"That bastard!" Diesel turned to Walker. "Only one spot left," She untied and shoved her mantis into her attachment pack. "Now what?"

126

Bull shouted from inside the Coliseum, "Move it, Diesel. Hustle."

"Go! Go, get inside, Diesel. While there's still time," Walker said, as Kali awoke and wiggled underneath him.

Diesel hopped on one foot to her friend, "But you'll die."

Walker smiled at her. "You go."

"But you will *DIE*, Walker."

(Don't cry. There's no crying in war.)

"Walker, I'm so sorry."

"No, Dee. I am." Walker thought of his frozen daughter, Nina. "Maybe this will finally make it all right."

Balancing, Diesel gave him a kiss on the cheek. Still kneeling, he pulled her down to him and hugged her hard.

"It's all about saving you, Diesel," Walker pushed her up gently. "Now, go before some other asshole takes your place."

Walker sighed and closed his eyes. Then he punched Kali in the back of the head. Dropping down, he bear-hugged the furious goddess, touching his throat to hers. He whispered in her ear, "When I blow, I'm taking you with me, sweetheart."

Seizing the opportunity, a gang of players stormed the stairs like a zombie horde. Bucking Walker off her back, Kali howled at the world with fiery rage. With time running out, Diesel scrambled for the finish line, hopping as fast and far as she could.

Diesel dove into a roll across the red laser line. "Number ten!"

Everyone's collars flashed for the last time. The PA system announced, "Diesel Duran is the last player to enter the Coliseum. This concludes the games. Thank you for playing."

All the drones lit in red and blue and sirens blared from everywhere. One flew into Diesel's face for the close-up reaction shot as she did a push-up. Bull offered her a high-five, but she broke down in exhaustion and collapsed at his feet. "It's over."

Bull offered his hand and helped her stand, "No, Diesel. It's just begun."

The Halo

Inside The Coliseum.

Diesel's collar stopped flashing white and finally turned blue. Angel stood in the shadows glaring at her as if his eyes could cast daggers. Back to looking beautiful, the bloody bride pranced next to Diesel's brooding nemesis and gave him a kiss on the cheek. The ghost guardian angel waved goodbye and then faded away. All the drones buzzed outside, ready to catch the next gore-filled shots.

(Of the losers.)

"Seventy-seven days of games, my ass. It hasn't even been half that long," Diesel snarked.

"Do not worry. *They* will find a way to keep the fight going. *They* always do." Cheng took her aside.

Outside, Walker screamed at the drones buzzing around his head, "This is prime time, baby!"

(He's going to die.)

Cheng rolled up one of his pant legs and stepped out of a dormant halo. "Take this and hide it, Diesel."

"What?"

Cheng slid the halo over the stump of her amputated leg.

Diesel flinched and pulled away. "Bad memories."

"Trust me. Walker got it right this time." Cheng smiled.

Diesel nodded and grimaced at the same time. When Cheng pushed the halo under her cut-off pants-leg, he noticed her green scaly knee-bud. "You are regenerating."

"I am?" Diesel touched the pinkish knobby growth. Three claw-like toes and a thick backward talon uncurled.

(It reminds me of a raptor.)

Unashamed, she showed him the reptilian foot that had sprouted out of her new double-jointed alien hybrid knee. Diesel wiggled her new toes for the first time. "I thought it was bad. Like cancer."

"That is not bad at all. Quite the contrary, it is excellent. The transfusion of my blood has activated the dormant DNA passed down by your father." Cheng smoothed his pant cuff to hide his smuggled halo.

"My Daddy?" Diesel flexed and pinched her claw-foot.

"Yes, Diesel. Your father was like me." Cheng pointed through the open arena to the sky. "We both came from Theta Rhonda Four."

"But you didn't know him?"

"No. I am sorry. I did not."

"I hate to break up this Hallmark moment," Bull interrupted from the breezeway as he pointed through the gate. "But everyone's about to lose their heads."

Outside The Coliseum.

Anticipating what would come next, Walker screamed at the drones outside, "This is prime time, baby!" He jumped onto Kali, determined to ride her piggyback. "You're coming with me."

Mr. Jerome Walker's rotting corpse appeared, doing an impressive tap-dance around Kali, scraping his shoes through her shadow. Ending with his arms open wide in a deep lunge, his jaw dropped and came unhinged on one side. Walker's ghost dad gathered his face together for a few last words, "So, here we are, Professor. Looks like *THE END*. Soon you'll be hanging out with me."

"From one hell to another," Walker growled at his father while clinging to the goddess.

"We can dance our miserable duet for all eternity."

"I'd say, 'kill me now,' but—"

Down the corridor, the collars of losing players vibrated and turned red-hot. Soon they'd all lose their heads, except for Walker, his collar stayed calm and cool.

"Uh, oh. You're still blue, Professor."

"What? *NO*. Come *ON!*" Walker scratched at his neck while managing to hang on to Kali. Everyone else panicked as their compliance collars burned into their skin. Swatting at the closest drone like King Kong atop the Empire State Building, Walker snagged one. He crammed his face into the webcam while screaming, "Come on. *KILL ME*. I want you to do it. Kill me!"

On cue, heads exploded in unison. Disappointed, Walker climbed off Kali. She untangled the chain from her legs and smiled at him as she pulled the spike from her foot. The goddess turned to face the lone survivor outside the Coliseum. She patted him on the head like a loyal dog. A drone followed to catch all the action.

"Nice show." She laughed. "You know I'm not permitted to harm you, Professor." Kali limped away amused.

"What the hell was that?" Walker whispered to himself.

Father zombie snickered, "I think you know."

The drone with a video display buzzed around Walker's head. On screen, the Master's smiling face conveyed a bizarre combination of adoration and mirth.

"Please. End this torture," Walker pleaded. "Just kill me, please."

No response came from the Master, only a look of idolization as his eyes glowed red.

Walker took a deep breath and then screamed at the drone, "Why won't *THEY* just let me *DIE?*"

The leader of the Bonanza blinked hard three times and then spoke in a loving tone. "Then what would TH-Th-They—" His voice skipped like a scratched record. "W-w-w-WE—" His head twitched twice as his processor auto-corrected. "What would TH-Th-th-th-th—" The Master seized. His face froze.

"Break loop," Walker commanded.

The Master relaxed. He took a deep breath.

"Rewrite auto-logical reference," Walker said. "We."

The Master nodded and finished his thought, "Then what would *WE* be, if *we* destroyed our creator?"

WHOA.

Will Diesel fight against the gladiators?

If so, how will she defeat Kali?

Will Angel get his vindictive wish?

What do *THEY* have planned for Walker?

—And—

What does Walker have planned for *THEY?*

All these questions, and more, answered in:

The Winners
Nevadaland Vol. 3

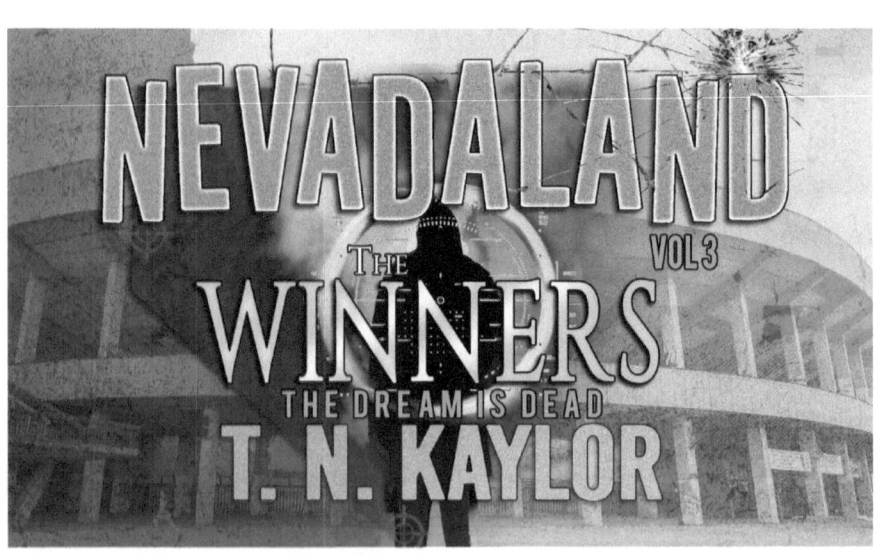

Coming October 6, 2017
In the meantime, enjoy DieselDuran.com
The Official Nevadaland Compendium

ABOUT THE AUTHOR

T. N. Kaylor lives in a "classified" location in Nevada where she weaves colorful characters into action-packed adventures with bizarre twists. As a child, timeless reruns of "The Twilight Zone" and "Alfred Hitchcock Presents" served as her black-and-white babysitter. Her earliest influences included Michael Crichton, Phillip K. Dick, and Agatha Christie. At age twelve, she wrote her first zombie story on wide-ruled notebook paper with a No. 2 pencil. As it circulated, she found the amazed reactions of teachers combined with the squealing delight of students to be powerfully addicting.

She has been writing ever since.

Over the course of her career, she has been a technical writer, a published academic, and a copy editor. Now, building on those literary skills, she injects her dark humor and twisted, visual imagination into gritty character-driven fiction set in surrealist dystopian worlds.

She has published many short stories in weird anthologies and fringe magazines. Popular in Japan, her collection of word art, *The Zen of Horror*, is now in its forth edition. Her superhero novella *Magnitude* features a magnetic battle against an immortal Vlad the Impaler. And for a dystopian apocalypse in progress, try the *NEVADALAND* series with mutant beasts, robots, and aliens that add an X-Files flavor to a dying alternate world.

Subscribe to the Official T. N. Kaylor newsletter at tnkaylor.com/subscribe for updates about new releases.

COOL F*CKERS PAGE

Here's a list of my top patrons that keep the vision alive. Join them on my Patreon creator page, pledge five bucks or more, and get listed on this page too.

Love you all!

Hunter Kaylor
Melva Mack
Jeni Barton
Ron Strong
Marian Sanborn
Kelly Ryan

THE *NEVADALAND* SERIES

THE PLAYERS *THE GAMES* *THE WINNERS*

02.14.2017   06.27.2017   10.06.2017

Did you miss one?

Don't worry, each volume of **NEVADALAND** is available on Amazon. There should be enough cyberpunk adventure to keep us all busy for quite a while! Meanwhile, check out DieselDuran.com for storyboards, drawings, forums, and more.

Support T. N. Kaylor on Patreon
patreon.com/tnkaylor

Follow T. N. Kaylor on Twitter
twitter.com/tnkaylor